BOOKS BY SANDY STARK-McGINNIS

Extraordinary Birds
The Space Between Lost and Found

EXTRAORDINARY
BIRDS

SANDY STARK-McGINNIS

BLOOMSBURY
CHILDREN'S BOOKS
NEW YORK LONDON OXFORD NEW DELHI SYDNEY

BLOOMSBURY CHILDREN'S BOOKS
Bloomsbury Publishing Inc., part of Bloomsbury Publishing Plc
1385 Broadway, New York, NY 10018

BLOOMSBURY, BLOOMSBURY CHILDREN'S BOOKS, and the Diana logo
are trademarks of Bloomsbury Publishing Plc

First published in the United States of America in April 2019
by Bloomsbury Children's Books
Paperback edition published in April 2020

Bloomsbury books may be purchased for business or promotional use.
For information on bulk purchases please contact Macmillan Corporate and
Premium Sales Department at specialmarkets@macmillan.com

ISBN 978-1-5476-0143-1 (paperback)

The Library of Congress has cataloged the hardcover edition as follows:
Names: Stark-McGinnis, Sandy, author.
Title: Extraordinary birds / by Sandy Stark-McGinnis.
Description: New York: Bloomsbury, 2019.
Summary: Eleven-year-old December waits to sprout wings and fly away,
until a new foster mother changes her perspective on home and family.
Identifiers: LCCN 2018045422 (print) | LCCN 2018051449 (e-book)
ISBN 978-1-5476-0100-4 (hardcover) • ISBN 978-1-5476-0102-8 (e-book)
Subjects: | CYAC: Foster home care—Fiction. | Birds—Fiction. |
Wildlife rescue—Fiction. | Orphans—Fiction.
Classification: LCC PZ7.1.S73765 Ext 2019 (print) | LCC PZ7.1.S73765 (e-book) |
DDC [Fic]—dc23
LC record available at https://lccn.loc.gov/2018045422

Book design by Jeanette Levy
Typeset by Westchester Publishing Services
Printed and bound in the U.S.A. by Berryville Graphics Inc., Berryville, Virginia
1 3 5 7 9 10 8 6 4 2

All papers used by Bloomsbury Publishing Plc are natural, recyclable products
made from wood grown in well-managed forests. The manufacturing processes
conform to the environmental regulations of the country of origin.

To find out more about our authors and books visit
www.bloomsbury.com and sign up for our newsletters.

To Summer and Sean
Love, always, Mom

1

At the third tier of branches my heart starts to beat fast. Birds need a fast heartbeat. It helps move oxygen through their bodies. Oxygen, lots of it, they need in order to fly.

There's always a point when I look down. It doesn't scare me, but seeing the green of the grass, and the gray of sidewalks, does make me think of gravity.

Karen is talking. It takes a lot of energy for her to use her "concerned" voice. I lean against the thickest part of a branch and take out my biography. There's a feather etched in the purple leather cover. I carry *Bird Girl: An Extraordinary Tale* with me wherever I go. No one's ever read it. It's my story, and it belongs to only me.

The best part about the book is I can turn to any page and be reminded of what I am, and where I came from. Like on page three:

Early in the morning, her mom had found a bird's feather lying on the kitchen floor. The feather was a sign. Less than an hour later, her mom gave birth to her. With icicles hanging from walnut trees in the orchard outside their house, her mom gave her a name.

"December, get down!" Karen yells. "You're not a bird," she says, like she knows my secret. "You're a girl, a human. You belong on the ground, where you're safe. If you had wings, I'd think you were some sort of evil spirit the devil made. Now come down out of that tree."

Karen talks a lot about Jesus and God, and told me God created everything and doesn't make mistakes. So why does she think if I had wings, I'd be an evil spirit instead of a beautiful creature?

"If you don't come down now, I'll have to send you back. Is that what you want?"

Yes, that's what I want. I can never stay in a house with someone who believes if I had wings I'd be evil. If she found out my secret, Karen would think she had to protect the world from a creature like me, and she'd lock me in a room with no windows and one door only she had the key to unlock.

I close *Bird Girl*, wrap it in a sweatshirt I never wear, and tuck it at the bottom of my backpack.

I keep climbing. I'm an amazing climber. When I grow up, I could, if I wanted, make my living climbing rocks and mountains, climbing the tallest tree in the world, which right now is a redwood tree growing somewhere in California. Its name is Hyperion and it's three hundred seventy-nine feet tall.

But a tree like Hyperion is not my flight tree. The tree I'm destined to take flight from is unique, but easier to find. Live oak trees grow everywhere around here. The hard part has been finding the right one. It will be an older live oak, its branches gnarled and twisting out and up, with lots of perfect places to build a nest. The tree, my flight tree, will stand by itself in a field somewhere, like it's been waiting for me all its life.

I'm getting better at ignoring being scared, the fast heartbeat, sweaty palms, the breathing. I don't have a choice. I am built to climb, but I was born to fly. I don't have much weight to carry, and I have bones that are light, but strong and flexible.

"You're going to fall!" Karen says. She's wearing an orange shirt. I don't like orange. It's the opposite of blue, my favorite color.

Of course I know I'm going to fall. That's how baby birds learn to fly. The first few times they try, they usually fall to the ground, but they learn they can make the impact easier by spreading their wings.

Karen wraps her arms and legs around the tree trunk, but she's built like a polar bear and doesn't get far. Even though polar bears aren't birds, they're still amazing creatures. They're born deaf and blind and grow to be one of the largest land animals on earth. So there's nothing at all wrong with being built like a polar bear, and I'd tell Karen this if she'd stop yelling.

"You're going to be in big trouble if you don't come down now!" If orange had a sound, it would be Karen's voice.

It didn't take me too long to notice that every time she got mad, a V formed between her eyebrows. It looks like half a bird claw. Even from up in the tree, I can see the V. She's real mad.

But I don't care. She shouldn't try to make me eat food that goes against my nature. I like seeds, sunflower more than pumpkin, and a little bit of meat. This morning I sat down at the table and poured myself a bowl of sunflower seeds instead of Cheerios and then Karen said something about how I was too skinny, and if I didn't eat more than seeds, that one day I'd "up and fly away."

Which is fine with me, but then she got another bowl, filled it with cereal and milk, and stood over me and said, "You're not going anywhere till you eat some real food."

I don't want to jump from too high. I'm not ready. But I have to keep challenging myself. Everyone's concerned about me getting hurt, that I'll break my arm, or leg. They shouldn't worry. I have a good idea of what I should and shouldn't do, even though most of the foster parents I've lived with would probably have something to say about that.

Like Susan and James. Every time they'd rake leaves and put them in a garbage bag, I'd spread them over the lawn again. The yard looked better covered in the reds and bright yellows of leaves than the dead color of grass.

Like Wes and Linda, where I felt like kicking a hole in the bedroom wall. Something had happened at school that day. A boy tripped a girl while we were playing soccer during recess. He did it just to be mean. I tripped him back, the yard duty person saw, and I'm the one that got sent to the principal's office. Wes and Linda punished me, too.

While Karen's trying to get me to come down, I read from *Bird Girl*, page eleven.

> December's wings are blue. She'll use them to fly to find a home. December's home will be a place where there are seasons, where in winter it snows, where in spring flowers are so bright they glow in the dark and birdbaths are always full from rain.

"Yes, hello." Now Karen is on her cell phone. "Yes, this is an emergency."

There are lots of ways to take off and fly. Birds can run into the wind and catch a current beneath their wings, or jump from someplace high and fall into the air.

Lately, I've been falling into the air. It's more dangerous, but the other way wasn't working.

"Just stay there until help comes!" Karen looks up, shielding her eyes from the sun. She wants to get a good look at me. Evil spirit or no evil spirit, deep in her soul she believes I'm an amazing creature.

I think about Amelia Earhart. I did a report on her last year, and I'll always remember reading three things that she said:

"Never interrupt someone doing something you said couldn't be done."

"You haven't seen a tree until you've seen its shadow from the sky."

And, "But what do dreams know of boundaries?"

Sirens are coming this way. A fire truck turns down the street where Karen lives. I'm the emergency.

"Dear Amelia Earhart," I whisper, "please give me the aerodynamics of thin bones, and feathers."

When it's time, I know the scar on my back will tingle and my wings will finally burst through my skin. I just need to step off the branch.

I will fly. Jumping into the air is the easy part.

2

I already know the first question Dr. S is going to ask. She likes "why" ones best.

"Why did you keep dumping the leaves in the yard?"

"Why didn't you tell the teacher about the boy tripping the girl?"

This time, "Why did you jump out of the tree?"

Pretty sure she already knows the answer to the questions before she asks, but she likes to get my take on them. Getting people to talk is what her job is all about.

"I didn't jump. My foot slipped and I fell."

"Karen said you jumped. Your feet were on the edge and you pushed off."

"Well, she was wrong. I was just standing up there. Maybe it looked like it to her. Karen makes a big deal over small things all the time. Dr. S, I don't want to jump out of trees, I want to climb them." Which is half the truth.

"You know, like how some kids like to play Legos, or with dolls. I like to climb trees. That's not that weird for a kid to want to do, is it?"

"Why do you want to jump out of trees?" She asks the same question a different way. Today Dr. S is wearing purple. Purple has blue in it, but I'm still not letting her trick me into telling her my absolute truth.

I might come close, so she won't ask me that question again. The story of my wings has to stay a secret. I'm only eleven, but I know a lot about the world. Enough to know I don't trust people knowing my secret. If they did ever see my wings, people would think I was crazy.

I also know enough about the world to not talk to Dr. S too much. I might say something I shouldn't, or something she can use against me. But saying nothing at all would be worse, and make it seem like I'm trying to hide things. Talking to Dr. S is like walking on a tree branch.

I'm lucky, though; I have natural balancing skills.

"I read in a book that Amelia Earhart used to climb trees when she was younger," I say.

"I didn't know that."

"That was one of my favorite things about her, so I remember it."

"I've read she once built a roller coaster." Dr. S has lots of certificates hanging on her wall to show how smart she is, but she knows this about Amelia Earhart because she has to find things that I will connect with. I do listen better when she talks about things I like. "One book said that when she rode it, she felt like she was flying. Do you feel like you're flying when you jump out of trees?"

"No, because I don't fly. I fall, like anyone else would."

"Would you like to fly?"

"In an airplane? Someday."

"Where would you go?"

I'd go to a place where it'd be hard to find me. "Antarctica."

"Why Antarctica?" We're back to a "why" question.

"It's the coldest continent on earth. Not a lot of people have visited there, but mostly I'd like to see a place not a whole lot of animals and plants call home."

"Interesting," Dr. S says. "I don't know if I'd want to visit Antarctica. I like being warm too much, and six months out of the year, the sun doesn't shine."

"So you visit the six months the sun does shine."

Dr. S nods. "True. Let's get back to jumping out of trees."

"I didn't jump. I slipped." I'm sticking to my story.

"Okay, let's say there's a person, a friend, who likes to jump out of trees. If he, or she, jumps out of them enough, do you think there's a possibility the friend will get hurt?"

This is a trick question because the answer is obvious, but Dr. S wants to test how I view real life. "Yes, there's definitely a chance of that happening."

Dr. S is quiet. She leans forward, her elbows perched on her knees like a bird inspecting prey. She's thinking hard about what to ask next, mapping questions that lead to what she wants to know from me before our time is up. If I had to guess, she's probably going to start asking about friends now. My having friends, or in my case, no friends, has been a concern of hers.

"If you could create a friend, how would that friend act?"

I was right. "Well, I guess they'd be a little like me," I say. "You know, Dr. S, you don't have to worry about me and the friend thing. The main reason I don't have any is because I don't stay in one place long enough."

Plus, if I'm going to fly away someday, what's the point of having friends?

Dr. S makes a bridge in front of her with her hands. This means she'll wait forever to hear the answer to whatever question she's going to ask. "Okay, let's talk about home. If you could live in any kind, what would it look like? Can you describe how it would feel?"

My house would be soft, and warm. It would be made out of plant fibers, mosses, and spiderwebs, just like a hummingbird's nest. At night, there would be someone there to tuck me under feathers, and I'd fall asleep, and that person would still be there in the morning.

"That person" won't be my mom, though. I used to live with her, and there was a time she took care of me. Her name was Samantha Lee Morgan. The only photograph I have of her is her kindergarten picture. She looks like a boy. Her hair's slicked back with too much gel and her front teeth are gone, but she smiles anyway. She's leaning forward, turning her face to the side, just a little, like she wants to run away.

She wears a muscle shirt, and on her shoulder is a tattoo of a black bird. I'd like to believe that even when she was five years old my destiny was written on her skin, like maybe my mom was born with the tattoo. Or that when she was a baby in the hospital, a bird flew into the nursery, its claws covered with ink. But the tattoo was temporary. Maybe she got it from one of those red toy dispensers that are by the door when you leave the grocery store. She'd probably been wanting to get something from one of the dispensers, and her mom promised to give her fifty cents if she was good.

I look a lot like my mom.

"A good foster home would . . . ," I start to say.

"It doesn't have to be a 'foster home.' It's your dream

home." Dr. S holds her arms out to the sides, like she would if she were trying to show me the wingspan of an albatross. "Think big."

Thinking big is imagining living someplace where I feel I belong. "I guess my 'think big' home would be somewhere I could stay for a long time. No one would yell. They'd treat me nice, and they wouldn't make a big deal about what I like to eat. And, no one would end up leaving me behind."

Dr. S puts her pen down, which means our time is up. "That's not too much to ask, is it?"

So far, life has taught me that it is, but I say "No" anyways because Dr. S is right, it doesn't seem like it would be too much to ask.

"One last thing." Dr. S hands me a bag of sunflower seeds. "For you."

I hold the bag against my stomach.

Dr. S closes our session with the same question as always. "Would you like to share anything from your book today?"

"Sure." My backpack is on the floor. I unzip it and slide my hand inside. I don't want to accidently pull out *Bird Girl*. Even though it's wrapped in a sweatshirt, it could still fall out, and Dr. S would see it.

I can never share *Bird Girl* with her. I can never share it with anyone. They might use it against me, as proof that

I should be locked away somewhere. Then, I would never get to fly.

But I am willing to share *The Complete Guide to Birds: Volume One*. It was a present from my mom. Inside the cover is an inscription that says, "*To December, Happy Birthday! Love, Mom.*" And then underneath, "*P.S. In flight is where you'll find me.*"

I push the guidebook across Dr. S's desk, and she opens it to a random page. "Three hundred sixty-four," she says.

I've memorized pretty much all the information in the book. If I had volume two, I'd memorize that, too. "The potoo. Potoos are also known as ghost birds. They're nocturnal. They feed on insects and small animals like bats and small birds. During the day the potoo stays motionless and can make itself look like a tree branch. It has feathers the same color as tree bark, and it has slits in its eyelids that allow it to be aware of movement even when its eyes are closed."

"So many amazing birds in the world." Dr. S pushes her chair away from her desk.

And I'll be the most amazing of all.

3

Adrian, my social worker, talks to Dr. S. If his voice were a color, it would be green. It's soft, and when he talks to me, I have to listen really hard. But I like his voice; it's what trees would sound like if they could talk.

I sit on the couch in the waiting room, open *The Complete Guide to Birds: Volume One*, then open *Bird Girl*, setting my biography inside the guidebook so that it's hidden from Adrian and Dr. S. I look over the part that reminds me of what I have to do to get back to my true nature.

ELEMENTS OF FLIGHT

<u>Weight</u> — December is naturally petite, and compact. Her bones are more birdlike than human. She has a nose instead of a beak, and, of course, she has teeth. Both will increase the force of weight.

Thrust — Birds have big sternums (bone in center of chest) where flight muscles are attached. In order for December to produce enough thrust to create forward motion, she'll have to become stronger.

Drag — December's wings, when they unfold, will naturally be smooth and lightweight. She'll have to worry about tucking her legs up against her body. However, she can learn to streamline. The more streamlined, the less drag.

Lift — December's wings will be big. Large birds, like the female Andean condor, can weigh up to twenty-four pounds and have a wingspan of ten feet. December's wings will be much bigger than that. She'll have to calculate what's called "wing loading" (weight divided by the upper surface of the wings) so she'll know how fast she has to fly to stay in the air.

    *Extra note (made by December herself):

    Right now, I weigh sixty pounds and have a wing/arm span of fifty-two inches. I can do forty push-ups without stopping. I can do

twelve pull-ups without stopping and can
hang from the bar for another two minutes
before having to let go. I am strong, but
need to get stronger.

A lot stronger.

After we leave, Adrian drives to Baskin-Robbins, which is where we go when he wants to have a serious talk. His reason for going to an ice cream shop: "The sweet balances the serious."

I don't hold anything back and order a triple-scoop banana split with Rocky Road, bubble gum, and chocolate ice cream, strawberry and hot fudge syrup, and extra whipped cream, with almonds on top. Almonds are the closest thing they have to seeds. Adrian doesn't think I can eat it all. I'm going to prove him wrong.

I dig my spoon into the almonds and whipped cream and push all the way down till I hit bottom, then open my mouth as wide as I can and shove everything in.

"I found a placement for you," he says. "There's always a chance it can become permanent." Adrian likes to believe he's giving me hope when he uses words like *permanent*.

But, synonyms for *permanent* are *eternal, lifelong,*

enduring. The word and all its synonyms are tricks. There is nothing that is permanent.

What he really means by *permanent* is being adopted, but even if that's what happens to me, getting adopted, it won't matter. Once my wings unfold, I'm flying away.

Adrian orders a single scoop of vanilla with no toppings. "I won't give up until we find a good home for you. You're not alone, December."

It's part of his job to convince me things aren't as bad as I think they are, or that everything's going to be okay. He's good at it. No matter how many foster homes I've been in, he tries to make me believe that the next one will be better.

The next one being better is not always true. I'd be hard to convince anyway. But I do believe in the possibility that each house will be my last, that my wings will finally unfold, and I won't need Adrian to find me a "good home" anymore.

Adrian hasn't taken one bite of his ice cream. He stares at it, and with his thumb and pointy finger squeezes the end of the pink spoon. "December, what do you think your life will be like ten years from now?"

What I want to say: *Well, my wings should be really strong, and I'll spend my days flying around the world, seeing every place there is to see. The end.*

Instead, I don't answer his question at all. "Did you know emperor penguins have the highest feather density of any bird? One hundred feathers for every square inch." I try to get Adrian's mind on something else. "It's to keep them warm. You going to eat your ice cream?"

But my subject change doesn't work. "I think you'd make a good scientist." He points the pink spoon at me. "Seven or eight years from now you could be in college, and be studying . . . What do you call the study of birds?"

"Ornithology."

"Yes!" Adrian lifts the spoon in the air like he's won something. He smiles in victory. "Wouldn't that be great? You would travel all over the world, studying different birds. Wouldn't that be an amazing life?"

"It would be amazing." I eat the last spoonful of whipped cream. Part of me thinks it really would be a good life, but the other part believes that this is what's even more amazing:

After I jumped from the tree in front of Karen's house, one of the EMTs checked to make sure I didn't have any sprains or broken bones. She said, "You have a little blood on the back of your shirt. Can you hold it up so I can take a look?"

There's always a quiet, a pause when people see the scar on my back. The EMT was no different. "You got scratched a little," she said, her voice whispering from the shock of seeing the twisted skin that covers the space between my shoulder blades. I know if I examine my scar closely, I will be able to see an outline of wings.

"It's just under your scar," the EMT said. I'd felt where the scratch was. A tree branch didn't cause it, though. It was caused by wings, beginning to break through my skin.

Here's another thing that's amazing: when I leaped from the tree, I was flying for six seconds. I counted, from the second my feet left the tree, to the second I started falling. "One one thousand, two one thousand, three one thousand, four one thousand, five one thousand, six one thousand."

I take the last bite of my sundae. I'm better at talking in half-truths than Adrian. "It would be amazing to study birds for the rest of my life," I say to him. But it would be more amazing to find my wings and fly.

Sometimes not telling the whole truth is the safest place to be. Plus, the thought of me going to college and having a normal life gives Adrian hope. Giving him hope makes him stop worrying about me, and he finally takes a bite of his ice cream.

4

Sometimes I practice holding my breath. Thirty-five seconds is my personal record. Birds have an advantage over humans. They have air sacs they use to keep air flowing through their lungs. Flying takes a lot of energy, so they need a lot of oxygen. I'll need a lot of oxygen, too. If I practice holding my breath, it will help build my lung capacity, and more lung capacity equals more oxygen I can breathe in, which equals more energy.

It feels good to be away from Karen's orange voice. I like this time between houses, riding in the car with Adrian, pretending we're going to my flight tree, where he'll drop me off and wish me "Safe travels."

My new foster home is out in the country. To get there we drive down a road that goes along a river and, every once in a while, through cottonwood trees, I see the muddy water.

Adrian turns into a driveway. There's a fence and pasture, but no cows or horses.

I can't see the color of the house. There's ivy growing over it. As we pull up and stop beside a green truck, I see river rock through the vines and leaves. The house is gray and brown with forest green trim.

There have been four houses I've lived in that have been painted a shade of brown, three a shade of green, three white, and one "canary" yellow. So far, I liked living in the canary yellow house best. It was easy to find, and I didn't have to memorize the address. I just had to look for the bright yellow color.

I slide my daisy suitcase out of the back seat.

Adrian carries the other one, plain blue, that holds my clothes. I like that everything I own fits into two suitcases and a backpack. It makes leaving for someplace fast and efficient.

I don't get butterflies in my stomach anymore. By now I'm used to standing outside a stranger's house, waiting for them to let us in and show me to my bedroom.

Adrian knocks, and I listen for footsteps. A part of me wonders, *What if those footsteps belonged to my real mom?* She'd be the one opening the door, and she'd be holding a cake with a lit candle for every year she had missed one of my birthdays.

"I'm here. I'm here!" the woman's voice almost sings.

Adrian told me her name. He also told me she lives by herself. I pictured an old lady with white hair, but Eleanor Thomas, my new foster mom, comes around the corner of the house wearing jeans covered in dirt and holding a shovel high in the air like she's trying to chase us away. She's wearing a brown cowboy hat, a brown vest, and brown rubber boots.

The saying "Never judge a book by its cover" is true, but the colors people wear have the same purpose as the color of birds' feathers—either for camouflage or to get other birds to notice them. I'd say, right off the bat, Eleanor is trying to blend in with her surroundings.

"Hope you haven't been standing here for too long. I was out back, trying to clean up the yard. I have a little garden. Planted asparagus, and it's looking really good."

If Eleanor's voice was a color, it would be between midnight blue and turquoise. I know my shades of blue.

Having a voice that's a shade of blue is a point in Eleanor's favor, I guess.

"It takes a few years for asparagus to grow," she says, "but mine will be ready this spring."

That's six months from now. I won't be here. But I don't like asparagus anyway.

"Asparagus is the favorite vegetable of the gods, you

know." Eleanor takes off her hat. Her hair falls over her shoulders. All the layers and strands remind me of tree roots.

I don't know what gods she's talking about. Every house where I've stayed had different ways of believing in God, and that was fine with me. I'm not sure about believing in God, but if someone were to ask me what, or who, God is, I'd tell them God has something to do with winter branches and feathers, and would look just like Amelia Earhart.

"Would you like to see the house?" Eleanor reaches for my daisy suitcase, grabbing it before I do. "I can take this for you."

Her voice is pretty, but I tell her, "I can get it myself."

"Okay." Instead of saying, "It's no trouble," and taking it anyway, she lets go of the handle. She leaves the suitcase for me to carry and makes a path of dirt footprints that lead to the front porch.

Part of being in a new foster home is getting a feel for the surroundings. Everything inside Eleanor's house is a shade of brown, too, the walls, the furniture, and all the posters and photographs she has of cowboys, both men and women. Weird, she doesn't have any pictures of family. Most people do, hanging in the living room or hallway. I would know. I always search them out and look for details. It's usually in their eyes. Whether they seem happy, sad, or if they're going to be mean like Wes and Linda. In every one of their wedding pictures, Wes had one of his fists clenched.

"You want to see your room?" Eleanor asks.

We walk down a short hallway. The room is bare except for a bed with white sheets and some blankets.

"I didn't know what you liked so I just left it plain. Feel free to decorate the way you want."

If I was staying for a long time, it would be nice to be surrounded by sky blue walls with white clouds and a tree painted on the ceiling. But I won't be staying.

We follow Eleanor back out to the kitchen. It smells like maple syrup and coffee. The only thing that's not brown in the kitchen is the green refrigerator. There's a newspaper article hanging on the front of it. All I can see is a photograph of a red-tailed hawk and the title "Rehabilitation Center, a Haven for Injured Animals."

Eleanor opens a door and takes us to the backyard. I've never seen anything like it. Five bird feeders hang from the porch, and two more hang from tree branches. Along paths leading around the yard are birdbaths. One shaped like a hand, one like a mushroom, another like a leaf, and two shaped like wings. Most of them don't have any water.

"Would you like to help me, December?" Eleanor's

holding a green bucket. "I have to fill them every week during the summer. Water evaporates fast."

As I fill two of the birdbaths, Eleanor and Adrian take care of the others. At the back of the yard, where one of the wing-shaped baths is, there's a red shed. As I'm pouring water, I stand on my tiptoes and try to look through a window. It's too dark inside to see anything. A blue jay lands on the roof of the shed, jerking its head side to side. It's probably waiting for me to leave so it can take a bath. "All right, I'm going," I whisper.

I take the bucket back to the porch and follow the path that leads to the other side of the yard. Eleanor and Adrian stand next to a garden. There are six rows of green-leafed vegetables. The last row are tomatoes, cherry, the only plant I know.

Eleanor picks a couple. "Would you like to taste one?" She holds the tomatoes out toward me.

"No, I don't like vegetables that much."

"I don't know if I did either when I was your age." Eleanor offers a tomato to Adrian. "But you can give gardening a try if you want. The maintenance part is not that much fun but the planting and harvesting is. So, whenever you want to come out here, you can. Sometimes I just sit here and watch things grow."

That does sound like an okay thing to do because I've

never sat and watched anything grow, except one time at school when we planted a sunflower in a plastic cup. We put them up on the windowsill in our classroom and checked on them every day. Through the plastic we saw white roots twisting and spreading at the bottom of the cup, and I thought that's what my wings were doing, too, twisting and spreading around my bones and muscles, the roots growing strong.

Adrian bends down close to me. "How do you like it so far?"

"I just got here."

"Eleanor knows a lot about animals. I didn't tell you this before, but I met her a few months ago. I'd found a baby opossum that was injured. I took it to a place where they help hurt animals, and there was Eleanor."

"Well, all I can say for sure right now is that I like her birdbaths."

"That's something, right?"

The blue jay I saw before is bathing in one of the wing-shaped baths. Scientists think birds take baths to keep their feathers healthy and functional. My mom left before she taught me how to take care of mine.

"I'm going to go now. I'll check in with you two in a couple days, to see how things are going." Adrian kneels down, but I'm still watching the blue jay. It fluffs its feathers and moves its wings in and out of the water. I know what Adrian will say next: "If you're not okay, I'll come get you." He says it every time.

"This is going to be good." He says this every time, too. And he'll say it again because he believes if he keeps saying it, one of these days he's going to be right.

We walk out a gate. Adrian shakes Eleanor's hand. "If you need anything, please call." He slides behind the steering wheel, and through the front window gives me a thumbs-up sign.

I hold up my thumb, and like I usually do, I think about how it might be the last time I see Adrian, because what if my wings decide to sprout from my scar. I won't have a chance to tell him I'm leaving, won't have time to even say goodbye. I'll just fly away.

I wave until Adrian's halfway down the driveway. Eleanor starts back toward the house before I do. As I turn to follow her, my eyes land on the back bumper of her truck. There's a sticker, "California Association of Taxidermists," and a picture of another red-tailed hawk next to the words.

I'm not sure what taxidermists and birds have in common, but I won't be sticking around here long enough to find out. I look up to wave to Adrian one more time, but he's gone.

I glance at the bumper sticker again. Both the words

and the picture of the hawk are the same color, brown, just like everything in Eleanor's house.

"I've been a member for a long time." Eleanor nods toward the sticker. "It's a hobby."

"Oh." I pretend like I'm not interested.

"Look!" Eleanor steps off the porch and points to the sky above the open field.

"It's a hawk."

"No." Eleanor shields her eyes from the sun. "Turkey vulture."

"They look majestic from here, but up close they're ugly."

"Guess *ugly* is how you look at the bird," Eleanor says. "They're amazing fliers. They can soar for hours without flapping their wings. And they're scavengers. I like to call them 'Nature's Garbage Company.' Even vultures have a purpose."

So, Eleanor knows about birds. It's at least one thing we have in common.

"Everything has a purpose," Eleanor says, still watching the turkey vulture.

"Maybe." I think she's looking at "purpose" through rose-colored glasses, though. It's not that everything has a purpose. It's more like purpose is about survival. When eagles soar way up in the sky, as beautiful and majestic as they look, they're searching for prey. And it's cool vultures can kill bacteria and toxins in their stomach, but they eat dead things off the ground, and over evolutionary time their stomach had to become stronger in order to survive. So, survival is the real purpose of every living thing.

And that's what I have to do now. Survive this foster home, like I've survived every other foster home, until I can fly away.

"It's almost dinnertime. I'm going to get you something to eat." Eleanor leans against the door, but doesn't open it. She's waiting for me to follow. She doesn't want to leave me by myself, out here, with all this open space and a sky wide enough to see mountains.

"I'm not hungry. I am tired, though. I'm just going to go to my room."

I wait for Eleanor to say something like, *You should really eat something. I went to the store and bought a lot of food, all for you,* but instead she says, "I'm sure it's been a long day. If you need anything, let me know."

In my room, I open my two suitcases and take out my six blue T-shirts, six pairs of jeans, and one blue pullover sweatshirt. I tuck them in spaces between my bed and the wall. The second suitcase is filled with my orphaned dolls. I lay them around my pillow.

Birds use all kinds of things to build their nests: twigs,

sticks, mud. Some use leaf strands, grass, and spider silk. The ruby-throated hummingbird decorates its nest with lichen to camouflage it from predators. What each bird uses depends on its environment.

Nests are meant to be temporary. Since I'm not a regular person, having a permanent home isn't important, but birds don't leave the nest until they can fly.

I take out *Bird Girl* and whisper-read, *"At December's house, the door was always left open. This is because December's mom wanted her to be able to fly out if she needed to. December did fly, but she only flew from walnut tree to walnut tree in the orchard behind where they lived. Her mom warned December not to go far. She taught December that if the world found out what she was, it wouldn't understand."*

Some birds can sleep with one half of their brains awake. It's called unihemispheric slow-wave sleep. It allows birds to sleep with one eye open so they can watch for predators.

At every foster home I've been to, I've practiced falling into unihemispheric slow-wave sleep. I sit up in my bed, close one of my eyes, and wait for sleep to come.

5

You ready to go?" I don't recognize Eleanor when I walk into the kitchen the next morning. She's dressed in a skirt and nice shirt that shines a little, and she's wearing makeup—pink lipstick, mascara, and blue eye shadow.

"How do I look?" She twirls around.

"You look like a peacock." This is a compliment. Peacocks are one of the most beautiful birds in the world. Many people don't realize, though, that the male peafowls are the beautiful ones.

"Well, thank you, December. They're noisy birds, too, and I hope to be noisy enough to persuade some people to give the wildlife refuge where I volunteer some money."

"Is that how you know about birds?" I feel the weight of *The Complete Guide to Birds: Volume One* inside my backpack.

"Well, my mom loved birds. She'd take me birdwatching all the time. She taught me all she knew. Sometimes I visit the schools around here, too. It gives me an opportunity to pass on to kids the knowledge my mom gave to me. You like birds, don't you?"

"Yeah." I wonder just how much Eleanor knows about birds. Does she know seagulls are great parents? Does she know the albatross has the longest lifespan of any bird? Or that one of the first birds on earth was the *Archaeopteryx*? "Do you know what the fastest flying bird is?" I ask.

"Hmm, the golden eagle?"

"No, it's the peregrine falcon." When it comes to knowing about birds, Eleanor's no match for me.

"What about you?" Eleanor slides her arm through her purse strap. "How do you know so much about birds?"

"I just like them. I like that they can fly."

"But why not airplanes, or helicopters? They fly."

"Birds were born to fly."

"True. I hope you'll be comfortable here, December. I'll do everything I can to make you feel like it's home."

Eleanor opens the door to leave, then turns around. She squints her eyes like she's trying to see through my T-shirt and jeans and skin to my light, flexible bones. "Won't you be cold? It'll be hot this afternoon, but the mornings are cool."

"No, I don't get cold." Not everything about me is written in my file. Things like, my resting heart rate averages five hundred beats per minute, not as fast as a hummingbird's, but faster than a chicken's, and I have an extra layer of skin that, when my wings unfold, will turn into feathers.

"I don't want you getting sick." Eleanor races to her room. "I have a jacket . . . It's brand-new. I'll be right back."

The jacket she brings back is fluffy and white with rainbow glitter on it. Nothing I'd ever wear in a million years. White is not my color, and the one word that describes my feelings about glitter is *gross*.

"Thanks," I say, and hold the jacket in my hand. "You know, you get sick from germs, not from being cold."

"That may be so, but it's still nice to be able to stay warm. Keep it in your backpack. Just in case."

In the bed of Eleanor's truck are two shovels, some wood, and a big toolbox. Eleanor backs out of the driveway. "I build houses, and do some repair work."

I build nests. Eleanor builds houses.

As we drive, she turns up the radio. "This is my favorite song. I was named after the woman that it's about, Eleanor Rigby."

Eleanor sings. She sings like no kind of bird I've ever heard. Her voice isn't beautiful, or bad. She doesn't shout above the singer, and she doesn't sing so low I can't hear her. It's just her voice, not pretending to be anybody else's.

We pull up in front of Fairview Elementary School.

The walls are painted swimming pool blue with twilight blue trim.

I've lost count of how many schools I've been to. I don't mind going. Most of the time it's a lot better place to be than a foster home.

"Adrian registered you already, so you should be set. Your class is in room eight. You want me to walk you?" Eleanor opens the door.

"No, I'll be okay." I grab my backpack.

"You sure? I better walk you."

"No, I'm used to this. It's not that big of a deal." I slide out of the truck.

"Okay, but if you need anything, don't be afraid to have the school call me. I'll be here." Eleanor grabs the jacket from the seat where I left it. "Don't forget this."

Goose bumps do form on my skin, but it's a natural reaction to the difference between the warmth of the car and the outside air. Eleanor waves goodbye, and as she drives away I can still hear her favorite song playing over the radio.

And even though Eleanor telling me to call her if I need anything is the nicest thing a foster parent has ever said to me, I still stuff the glittery white jacket inside my backpack.

Room eight is at the end of the hall, the last classroom

before the playground. The door is closed and the lights are out. There's a pile of backpacks against the wall, but I keep mine with me and walk outside across the blacktop to a deep green leafy tree. I unzip the pocket with the owl pin on it and take out *The Complete Guide to Birds: Volume One.*

The dwarf cassowary lives in New Guinea on steep hills and in forests. Scientists have found they're very hard to spot in the wild. On the first day at a new school, if I could, I'd change myself into a dwarf cassowary. But it seems there's no amount of camouflage that could make me disappear so that I could sit in a classroom, or wander a playground, unnoticed.

I hear singing. *"I asked my mother for fifty cents, to see the elephant jump the fence. He jumped so high, he touched the sky, and never came back till the Fourth of July."*

The girl jumping rope is wearing pink rain boots with a jacket to match. It's the end of September, and there aren't any clouds in the sky. We usually don't get rain for another couple of months. The pink is a big exclamation point standing out against the morning.

When she's finished with the elephant rhyme, she says another. *"Black birds, black birds, sitting on a wire. What do you do there? May we inquire? 'We just sit and see the day, we just flock and fly away. By one, two, three . . .'"*

A group of girls glides across the playground. They're wearing even brighter clothes than the girl jumping rope, lots of lime green and fluorescent pink. A few have bows. Some have their hair braided. One has pigtails that bounce. They look mean. It's the way their arms are folded across their chests, and how their noses are pointed to the sky. If anyone gets in their way, they won't notice; they'll run them over with their pink glittery boots.

They glide across the blacktop and float into the bathroom.

The girl jumping rope starts the black bird rhyme over, but when she gets to *"May we inquire?"* she looks over at me. "You're new. What's your name?" she asks, swinging the jump rope over her shoulder. "I'm Cheryllynn."

I open my book, trying to ignore her. Making friends has never made sense to me.

"You don't want to talk? Too bad, because I'd be a very cool friend to have." Cheryllynn lets the jump rope fall from her shoulder and catches it before it hits the ground.

Just because she's trying to get me to talk to her doesn't mean we have to become friends. "That song you were singing, about the black birds . . ." I close the book. "There are several species of black birds that live in America—which species is the song talking about? There's the raven, the Brewer's blackbird, the red-winged blackbird, the . . ."

Cheryllynn has a confused look on her face. "You know a lot about animals?"

"Mostly birds."

She bends down next to me. Her eyes are dark brown, her skin the color of bark on a paperbark maple tree. "I don't know much about birds, but last year our class went to the river to see the salmon. The males and females were swimming upstream to lay and fertilize their eggs. They looked really beat-up. You know the salmon die after laying their eggs? The babies are on their own as soon as they're born."

I feel my eyebrows rise a little. Her knowing about salmon is a surprise. "Well, some animals don't need their moms and dads to survive," I say. "We do. It'd be cool if humans could just start walking right when they're born, but we need someone to help us."

Birds are different. Some hatch from eggs with their eyes open and already have down feathers. They leave the nest anywhere from a few hours to seven days after being born. But birds that hatch with their eyes closed, like owls and hawks, need their parents longer. They stay in the nest for as long as two hundred seventy days.

The group of girls I saw earlier glides back across the playground. "Hey, Charlie!" one of them yells. She's wearing the brightest of the bright clothes. "Sorry, I mean . . .

What's your name again?" Her voice is more orange than Karen's.

The girls move like a flock of starlings, turning in unison as they slide over the blacktop, away from us. Cheryllynn stands up with her fists clinched.

"Who's 'Charlie'?" I ask her.

"That was my old name. Now I'm Cheryllynn." She sits against the tree trunk next to me. "What's your name?"

"December," I whisper.

"That is an amazing name."

"Yes, it is." I have to take out the glittery jacket to get my bird book into my backpack.

"Where'd you move from?"

"Everywhere."

"Wow! Everywhere?" I can't tell if Cheryllynn is making fun of me or if she believes me about moving from "everywhere."

"Just so you know, I'm a foster kid, and the lady I live with is not my mom. Is there anything else you want to know?"

Cheryllynn takes a necklace made of Froot Loops out of her rain jacket pocket. "Yeah, I want to know if you want some Froot Loops. I made the necklace myself."

They are colorful, like feathers on a rainbow lorikeet. "No thanks. I don't eat cereal." I start walking toward my classroom, hoping the bell will ring and Cheryllynn will have to line up for class, and she'll stop trying to be my friend.

"Well, where do you live?" She follows me. "We might live close to each other, and we can hang out after school." Right now, Cheryllynn is a harpy eagle. Their talons can wield a crushing grip of one hundred pounds or more, and I feel like I'm caught in one of them.

If I tell her what she wants to know, maybe she'll stop following me. "I live with a lady named Eleanor. She lives out in the country in a rock house with vines growing all over it."

"You live with the taxidermist?" Cheryllynn asks.

Taxidermist, there's that word again.

"I know exactly where that house is." Cheryllynn walks right next to me. "The woman. She came to school to do a presentation. She was with the wildlife refuge. It's by the river. They take care of hurt animals."

Suddenly a ball comes flying by. "Watch out!" a boy yells. He dribbles a basketball around us, and we shuffle our feet off the court.

Cheryllynn keeps talking about Eleanor. "She brought a raccoon, a fox, but mostly birds—an owl, two different kinds of hawks. She told us they were going to be ready to set free soon. You know people around here call her the 'Bird Whisperer'?"

"She can talk to birds?"

"Well." Cheryllynn opens her pocket, probably to see if any pieces of cereal are left. "There are two versions of the Bird Whisperer story. You want to hear the good one, the bad one, or both?"

"Both."

The bell rings. Kids are running around us.

"The good one is that birds make their way to her when they're hurt—a broken wing, ate something poisonous—or, some say, birds go to her when they're sad, like if one of their babies has fallen out of a tree or is not able to fly and dies. The bad story is she has a way of calling healthy birds to her with a whistle or a song. When they come to her, she stuffs them and sells them to people."

The scar on my back tingles. My heart beats like hummingbirds' wings.

"That's all I know about the lady." Cheryllynn takes one more bite of her necklace and moves toward the door, yelling, "Maybe I'll see you at lunch! We can talk more then, if you want!"

I've heard all I need to know about Eleanor. I can't move.

Taxidermists stuff animals. They stuff birds. I've worried about being captured, but I've never imagined being stuffed.

Eleanor's a taxidermist, and I live with her.

A yard duty lady blows a whistle at me. "Young lady! The bell rang! You need to line up!"

I'm the only one standing on the playground, just like I'd be the only bird of my kind Eleanor would have a chance to stuff, if she ever finds out about my wings.

6

In front of the school at the end of the day, I sink against a fence and open my bird book. Now I know why Eleanor sang this morning. She can't help it. I'm not going to be lured by her song, though.

Over the top of my book, I see Eleanor's truck. I live with the Bird Whisperer.

"December." Eleanor does have a nice voice, a voice just right for making someone believe she would never hurt them.

Tomorrow when I see Cheryllynn I'm going to tell her thank you for saving my life.

"December?" The truck door closes, and her boots scratch the sidewalk. "You ready to go?"

I hold my bird book close to my chest and make sure I walk behind Eleanor. She tries to open the door for me. "No, I can do it."

Music plays on the radio, and I reach over and turn it off. "You don't like the music?" Eleanor asks.

Hummingbirds, penguins, and hawks are some birds that don't sing, but most birds do, and the types of songs they sing have to do with their age, whether they're male or female, and where they live. Birds that live in the forest use short calls, because sound can ricochet off trees or be taken in by leaves.

Eleanor is not a bird, obviously, but she must have learned what songs attract them. She stands outside, day or night, and sings the "Eleanor Rigby" song, her soft voice traveling miles, the vibration picked up by birds, which fly to her backyard. They eat until they're full, and then take a bath, cleaning their feathers, and when the birds are at their most vulnerable—fed, cleaned, and sleepy—Eleanor catches them in a net.

"How was school today?" she asks.

Crows usually don't sing. They call, to warn other crows to stay away.

"It was fine."

"So you had a good day?"

"I said it was fine."

The superb lyrebird has one of the loudest calls of any bird, but the bittern bird has one of the farthest traveling.

Eleanor pulls to the side of the road and rests her hands on the steering wheel. "You don't seem like you're okay."

"I'm fine." I slap my bird book closed. "Everything is fine."

Eleanor pulls onto the road again. The rest of the way home, I wait for her to start whispering.

When we get to the house, I tell Eleanor I'm going to my room to do homework. I set my backpack and bird book on the floor. Eleanor's going to start singing. At first, it'll be soft, like a lullaby, but soon it'll grow loud enough for the vibration to float under my door and try to hypnotize me.

I tiptoe down the hallway to see where she is. I peer around the corner, into the kitchen. Eleanor sets a pot on the stove, then walks to the refrigerator. She's starting to cook dinner.

Using the front door is too risky. I look across the living room. There's a window Eleanor's left open. She must not've read everything that's in my file, because there's a "To-Do" list foster parents need to follow before I live with them, number one being "Make sure windows and doors are secure. You'll want to discourage easy access to an exit."

Soon as I'm outside, I run to the shed in the backyard. There's a latch where a lock should be. I have a feeling this is where she does her work on birds, and I want to know what I'm up against.

Inside, it smells like dust and chemicals Eleanor must use for taxidermy. On a table there are tools and a couple lamps. This is definitely the place where she stuffs animals. They're displayed on a shelf, all birds, perched on wooden pedestals. I count them. Three crows. Two robins. A great horned owl, and one red-tailed hawk. Up close, their eyes shine. I stroke the owl's feathers, and I swear it twitches a little, like it's remembering how it used to fly. I take it off the shelf, dust floating from its feathers, and cradle it in my arms.

I'm going to call the owl Teresa, after Saint Teresa of Ávila. Karen used to take me to church all the time, and she really loved saints. At dinner, she would choose a saint to talk about. My favorite was Saint Teresa because Saint Teresa was rumored to have powers of levitation, which is as close as a human gets to flying without the help of machines, or, in my case, wings.

I close the door to the shed. Before climbing back into the house, I make sure Eleanor isn't calling my name. She isn't, but she is singing. I try not to pay attention to her song as I lean over the windowsill, setting Teresa on the floor.

The singing stops, and I hear footsteps walking across

the kitchen floor. I pull myself inside and hide behind a couch.

Peeking my head over the armrest, I see Eleanor standing in the hallway. "December? Dinner is almost ready."

She turns back to the kitchen, and plates clank together. She's setting the table.

I grab Teresa and take her to my room. I set her on the bed, against the wall with my clothes and orphaned dolls. "I don't know what your life was like, but I can guess what happened to you." I lie on the bed and stare into Teresa's empty, glassy eyes. "Eleanor probably set a trap for you. She went to the pet store and bought some mice. Went out to her backyard at midnight and got some chicken wire and used it to build a little corral. She set the mice free, and then waited, with a net, for you to swoop down and grab one. And that, Teresa, was the end of you."

I stroke her feathers, and hold up *Bird Girl*. "I know I look human, but I'm not really. I mean, I am, but I'm part bird, too. And one day, I'll be all bird."

"Look." I open my biography and show Teresa a sketch of the birdlike me. "See my wings?" I turn the page and read to her: *"The weeks after December was born, she would perch on her mom's shoulder, and they would walk through the walnut orchard. Her mom would hum, and December would sing her song, but when her song got too loud, her mom would put her finger on December's beak and say, 'You have to sing quietly. I don't want anyone ever to take you from me. If you promise to sing quieter, I will let you fly around the orchard a few times.' So December sang, but softer, spread her wings, and zigzagged through the trees."*

I close my biography. "If I would've stayed more like a bird, maybe my mom wouldn't have left me. She got to where she was afraid of . . . everything." I stroke the feathers on Teresa's wings. "I'm not afraid of anything, though. Well, I wasn't until I came here, and now I have to make sure I don't end up like you."

"December?" Eleanor is right outside the door.

"Coming." I'm nose to beak with Teresa. "I know she's the one who did this to you," I say, and hope Teresa's owl friends that are still alive hear me, with their amazing auditory systems. "I'm going to have to hide you, okay?"

I put my biography and Teresa in the back corner of the closet and grab my bag of sunflower seeds for dinner.

At the kitchen table, I notice Eleanor has set places for both of us. There are two glasses of water. She's given herself a fork, but not me. I just have a plate. We're sitting next to each other.

I slide my plate and water to another spot, on the other side of the table from Eleanor, and reach into the bag of seeds. When Eleanor sits down, she doesn't say anything about me moving. She takes a bite of her spaghetti and closes her eyes like the spaghetti is the best-tasting spaghetti in the world. I wait for her to start talking about everyday things. This is what foster parents do. They think it helps take my mind off the fact that I'm really living with strangers. But Eleanor isn't talking at all. She keeps her eyes on her spaghetti and doesn't even look at me as she takes a drink of water. She looks out the window instead, probably keeping a watch out for birds.

The only sound is the crack of my sunflower seed, the *pooof* when I spit the shell, and the flat *click* as the shell hits my plate. Maybe Eleanor is thinking about where she's going to display me once I'm stuffed. She won't keep me in the shed. That would be a waste.

"How long have you been eating only seeds?" Eleanor asks, twirling spaghetti on her fork. It looks like a clump of worms.

"I eat other things sometimes, too. I just like seeds best." I'm going to have to hide my sunflower seeds. She could spread them across a glue trap.

Eleanor squints her eyes at me and nods. For every bite of spaghetti she takes and swallows, I crack and eat five sunflower seeds.

I'm not sure yet what kind of bird Eleanor would be. I've identified many of my foster parents as snowy owls.

Snowy owls have razor-sharp talons that could easily attack a human's head and eyes, though they've never been known to kill anyone. But Wes was definitely a southern cassowary, the meanest bird. It has razor-sharp spurs that can slice things open, and it has a strong kicking force. If someone's ever out in New Guinea or Australia and they come across a cassowary, it's a good idea that they turn around in the opposite direction and avoid contact. That's what I would do with Wes, too. Whenever I'd see him sitting alone in a room, I'd turned around and walk the other way.

Eleanor is going to be hard to figure out. On the surface she doesn't seem like she falls into the Top Ten Birds Most Likely to Kill Humans, but if she's capable of doing what she did to Teresa, who knows what else she'll do.

I think the hardest part of trying to stuff me will be getting me to fall for her trap.

"Did you get enough to eat?" Eleanor asks. "I know you really like seeds, but I have apples. Would you like one?"

I nod. "Sure." Apples grow on trees, at least. I'll eat the apple while I try to gather as much information on Eleanor as I can. "Have you had foster kids before?" I ask.

"No, you're my first." She sips some water. "I had a . . ." Eleanor takes her plate to the sink, grabs an apple from the refrigerator, and slices it up into pieces for me. "I met Adrian at the refuge, and he said he thought I would be a good foster mom. I've loved doing presentations at schools—interacting with the kids. I told myself, Why not? I hope you'll be happy here, December."

"I had a . . ." What was Eleanor going to say?

I get up from the table, dump my shells in the garbage, and wash my plate.

"I can do that." Eleanor shovels spaghetti into a glass bowl. "You can just leave it in the sink."

I leave the plate, but I'm used to cleaning up after myself. I don't want to be a burden, and I've always wanted to show my foster parents I can take care of myself, that I don't need them. They're just here to give me shelter, and if I had to, I could give myself that, too.

Eleanor starts singing. It's the same song. Maybe she doesn't know any other. The one she sings has worked in bringing birds to her, so why should she change it?

As I leave the kitchen, Eleanor says, "After I'm finished cleaning up, I'd like to take you to the wildlife refuge. Some of the animals need to be fed, and I want to introduce you to Henrietta."

"What kind of animal is Henrietta?" I ask, but I already know Eleanor's answer.

"She's a bird."

Of course.

7

The Wildlife Rehabilitation Center is farther out in the country than Eleanor's house. We drive along the river, and the land opens till the only things to see are the shadow of the Sierra Nevada Mountains in the distance and patchy specks of light.

It doesn't take too long to get there. When I step out of the truck I expect to hear injured birds squawking, but the only sound is the chirping of crickets.

The building looks like a regular house where somebody used to live. There's a yellow porch light shining above the front door, and there are tall, skinny trees surrounding the property. They look like guards, protecting the hurt animals.

The center is locked, but Eleanor has a key. "Henrietta is a red-tailed hawk. She had an operation to fix her wing, but we're having a hard time building trust with her. And we need to build trust so we can start the process of getting her to fly on her own."

Eleanor turns on a lamp, and inside a cage right by the door is Henrietta. Her feathers are deep brown, mixed with shades of bronze, and on her tail the feathers are a cinnamon color. She has a fierce-looking face, with her sharp beak and eyes set on the sides of her head. Her binocular vision helps her be an efficient predator. I've never been this close to a hawk.

I lean closer to the cage. Henrietta is so still, she looks like she could be one of Eleanor's stuffed birds. "I've seen birds like you flying in the air," I whisper, "but you're pretty amazing up close, too."

"Someone found her by the river, on the ground," Eleanor says. "She's lucky a coyote or raccoon didn't get her. The person said she checked to see if there was a nest around, but couldn't find one. That's good. Means there weren't any babies she had to take care of."

Eleanor slides her hand into a see-through glove, the kind doctors wear when they're doing surgery. She opens a carton of chicken gizzards and uses tweezers to pick up a piece. She opens the cage and dangles the piece of gizzard in front of Henrietta. "She won't take it, but watch."

Eleanor drops the piece of raw meat on the cage floor. Henrietta jerks her head and grabs the gizzard with her beak. "We've been trying to get her to take food from us since she got here. No one working here can establish a bond strong enough so that Henrietta will take food straight from their hand."

"Not even you?" Eleanor is supposed to be the Bird Whisperer.

"Nope."

Eleanor goes back to where there's a small refrigerator. I lean into the cage again and look Henrietta in the eyes. "What about me?" I ask Henrietta.

I'm careful not to move too fast, and back away from the cage. "Eleanor, can I try to feed Henrietta?"

"Okay," she says, like she was waiting for me to ask. Eleanor gives me a glove of my own and hands me the container of gizzards and the tweezers.

I open the cage door and grab one piece of meat. My hand floats toward Henrietta. She twitches a little. I hold the meat in front of her, and she seems like she wants to take it.

"Henrietta," I whisper, "you're an amazing bird, and I know you'd like a juicy mouse or some other rodent to eat, but this is what I have right now. If you fly again, then you'll be able to hunt all the mice you can catch."

Henrietta is being cautious. "I understand," I tell her. She snaps her head forward and snatches the meat.

"Oh, my." Eleanor watches Henrietta swallow the gizzard. "This is very good. Let's try something else."

I give the tweezers back to Eleanor and this time hold a piece of meat.

"Now"—Eleanor holds a piece of meat, too—"pinch it with the tips of your fingers. Be careful. Soon as Henrietta pecks at it, let go of the gizzard, letting it drop or letting her take it."

I dangle the food in front of Henrietta. She shuffles her claws backward.

"You're an amazing bird," I say again, and Henrietta grabs the chicken.

Behind me, Eleanor claps one time and raises her arms. "Woo-hoo!" She holds out her hand for me to shake. "Congratulations, December, you're officially Henrietta's trainer. You're going to get her to fly. Are you up for the challenge?"

Before I can think about what it really means to be in charge of training a bird how to fly, I take off my glove, shake Eleanor's hand, and say, "Yes."

Tonight, I carry Teresa to my bed and lean her against the wall. I get a little scared thinking about being Henrietta's teacher, but as I stare into Teresa's eyes, I think maybe Henrietta and I could learn to fly together.

But what if getting me to train Henrietta is part of a trap, an elaborate plan by the Bird Whisperer to capture me? We'll be out in a field releasing Henrietta, and the second she flies away, I'll be entangled in a net.

I tap Teresa on the beak. Maybe tonight while I sleep she'll coo advice about how not to get caught by Eleanor. *It's really not that hard,* she'll say. *You already know she's the Bird Whisperer, so now you just need to be aware of anything she's doing or saying that could be used in preparation for your capture.*

You'll eventually have to escape. If you have nowhere to go, there is a group of owls. They used to be my family. They don't live too far from here. They will be suspicious of you at first, but then once they see you won't hurt them—you won't, will you?—they'll let you live with them. You'll have to learn to hunt in the dark, you'll have to learn to live off mice—or, on a good day, a rabbit or a squirrel—and you'll have to learn to sleep in trees. But you will eat, and you'll be safe. That's all that matters, right?

I close my eyes. For the most part, Teresa is right—having food and a place to sleep are things that matter. But the thing that matters most is not that I feel safe in a foster home, it's knowing, if I have to, I can survive anything.

8

Owls' wings were designed for quiet flight, so this morning I'm like Teresa. I glide through the house, to the open window. If Eleanor caught me sneaking out, she'd have every reason to keep me inside. She'd only let me out to go to school, to fill birdbaths, or to train Henrietta. I take a chance, though.

I breathe in cold air, then breathe some more, and hold my arms out to the side, just in case I'm lucky enough to catch a current of wind.

Soon as I get to the river, I start digging. I find angleworms first. A little deeper into the ground are night crawlers. I've never seen them so big.

On the way back to the house, I don't run. I hold the worms, one hand cupped over the other. They are precious creatures I will try to eat later. The thing about becoming a bird is I have to adapt myself slowly. There are other things that birds eat, depending on where they live: fish, shellfish, crickets, mosquitoes, and seeds. But I figure if I can eat worms, I can get used to eating anything, if I need to.

There's light coming from one of the windows. Eleanor is awake.

"December?" Her voice is coming from the back of the house. "Oh, I've lost her already," I hear her say.

I know it's mean, but I don't answer. Part of me kind of likes the sound of Eleanor calling my name. She says, "December?" in her singsong cadence, and I have to remind myself her voice is dangerous. What's worse is, if I had to give her voice a color, the color would still be a shade of blue.

I listen to her blue voice call me. There's a pause between her "Decembers." Eleanor's waiting for me to call back. She says my name four times, and all I can do is act like a stuffed version of December Lee Morgan, aka Bird Girl. After the fourth time calling my name, she starts whistling, trying another type of call to get me to come to her.

I pull myself through the window.

Usually people keep ziplock bags in a drawer by the kitchen sink or by the stove. I start with the drawers by the stove. The third one has what I need. I slide the worms into a bag and close it halfway. They need to breathe. Dead worms probably don't taste as good as live ones.

I'll squish the worms if I put them in my pocket, so I go to my room and set them behind my backpack.

I return to the kitchen and through the back door, I see Eleanor, carrying a bag of birdseed. "December?"

This time I answer. "I'm here."

"Feel like I keep losing you." She unhooks a bird feeder and fills it with some birdseed.

"I'm not lost. I'm right here."

"So you are," Eleanor's brown hair is pulled back in a ponytail this morning. Her eyes are close to the same shade of brown as mine, her skin the same light shade. "You want to help me fill the rest? Weather's starting to change, so filling the bird feeders is a tradition for me."

So is stuffing great horned owls. I think of Henrietta. If she doesn't learn to fly, Eleanor might stuff her, too. She'll display us in the living room, side by side. We'll be special. We'll have labels on our pedestals, like they have in museums, with the Latin form of our names. I don't know what Henrietta's would be, but mine would be *avis puella*, "bird girl." Eleanor will choose brown for our glass eyes, as close to our original shade as possible, and clean our feathers, making them shine so that all the different shades of blue, for mine, and browns and reds, for Henrietta's, can be seen.

"I have some birdhouses that are broken," Eleanor says

as she hands me the birdseed bag. "I'd like to fix them up in the next couple days, and hang them up. Maybe you'd want to help me do that, too?"

"You should get some feeders for hummingbirds. Did you know they eat one hundred percent of their body weight every day?" I take the bag.

"Yes, and right now they're eating twice that much, fueling up for their migration. That's a good idea."

Eleanor probably has to pay lots of attention to migration routes. It gives her an idea of what kinds of birds might be flying over her property this time of year.

I set the bag of seeds on the ground. While Eleanor is examining two broken birdhouses, I peek through a hole in the fence.

And then I see a tree in the middle of a field, a live oak, the one I've been looking for. From here, it's perfect, and I have to take a couple deep breaths because it's so beautiful. The branches are curved and thick, creating twisting and meandering paths to where the sky begins. I was starting to believe I would never find it, but here it is, growing for who knows how long, a hundred years maybe, behind the Bird Whisperer's house. It is the perfect tree for climbing, too. The first tier of branches is within arm's reach, easy for pulling my whole body up and over. It will be like climbing a ladder.

"Eleanor, can I go out there for a little bit?" I point toward the fence.

"But you have to get ready for school."

"I won't go far."

"Just for a few minutes, then. If you're gone for too long, I'll call you."

I'm sure she will.

This morning the clouds in the sky look like wings, but they always look like wings to me. I look back at Eleanor's house and wonder if she's watching me through a hole in the fence.

I don't throw birdseed on the ground until I'm halfway between the fence and my tree. It's far enough away so birds have a chance to eat, then fly away before Eleanor can catch them.

In the distance is a line of cottonwood trees, growing by the river. Above the trees, starlings take flight against the sky and form a sphere, a flying bird ball that stretches into a tube, moving like a wave.

I throw more birdseed over my shoulder and stand at attention when I'm close to my tree. Grass and weeds have stopped growing two feet from the trunk, and in the space between is dirt, as though the tree is royalty and the other plants have made room to display its beauty. I set the bag of birdseed on the ground and look up through the tree.

I want to feel its branches, so I pull myself up to the lowest tier, letting my feet dangle in the air. In the field where I first threw the seeds, a bluebird is pecking at the ground. Another bluebird joins it, but they don't have a chance to feast for long. A crow lands, fluffing its feathers, trying to intimidate the others, telling them all the seeds belong to him. They fly away, but they'll find food somewhere else. They'll go on surviving.

I pull my feet up and balance myself on the branch. Like it always does, the skin under my scar starts to tingle. Holding my arms out to the side, I shape them like wings as best I can. Birds' wings are all different, depending how they use flight to survive. Seabirds' wings are long, narrow, and flat, and are built for long journeys across the ocean. Birds that need to take off fast, like pheasants that spend most of their time on the ground, have short, broad wings. My wings will have to fly long distances and be built to make quick takeoffs.

"One," I count, "two . . ."

Henrietta.

There's a chance if I do jump, I could break my ankle, or wrist. Spraining either might cause me not to be able to train Henrietta. I'd be the wounded one. And if I can't help Henrietta, and I'm the one she trusts, then I'll have increased her chances of becoming a stuffed bird.

But if I get stronger, and fly, Henrietta and I will have the chance to soar together, side by side.

I will fly. ". . . three." I have jumping down to a science, taking deep breaths, inflating my lungs, hoping they act like balloons, and bending my knees, using my thigh and calf muscles to push off the branch.

I've done this enough times that I've taught myself, in midair, to be aware of waiting. When my wings do unfold, I want to know the second they push out of bone and skin and spread across the air. I want to be able to remember that moment.

But, this time, the moment doesn't come, and I fall to the ground. Sometimes the ground is hard, sometimes it's wet, sometimes it's soft, and sometimes it isn't filled with hurt at all, just a mouthful of dirt.

I don't get up right away. It's nice to breathe in the smell of leaves, and roots, and of things growing, and I try to convince my bird self that the ground is not such a bad place to be.

From this perspective, Eleanor's house, with its vines spreading over the roof and around the walls, looks like it's becoming part of the earth, like the plants are on a mission to slowly take over the windows, too, and make their way inside, the vines twisting around couches, chairs, the refrigerator, and my ankles, making sure all things stay planted.

When I believed my bird type was more like a loon's, I focused on taking off from the ground. The last time I tried was my eleventh birthday. I used a birthday wish for extra support, and right before I jumped into the air I imagined blowing out candles. One wish was all I needed for my wings to unfold.

But the potential for birthday wishes to come true is either a big lie or it depends on the wish, or the person, or life in general, or a combination of all three. Lesson learned from that experiment: one day is as good as any to find the possible.

Eleanor will be calling my name pretty soon. I put one foot back and lean over my front knee. Every once in a while, I have to try this way of flying, just in case.

I want to keep my head down until I have enough momentum. I'm almost at full speed. My heart beats in rhythm with a different life, a life where I won't have a scar anymore.

Out of habit, I make a wish anyway. I wish for the aerodynamics of thin bones, and of feathers, and I leap into the air, spread my arms out to the side, and try to feel wind against my skin as air lifts me up.

But I fall. There's the smell of wet dirt and roots again, trying to remind me with every breath I'm just a girl, a human, and the ground is where I belong.

"December?" Eleanor's voice is a little shaky. She's afraid I've run away.

"Coming!" I brush dirt off my jeans and run to get the bag of birdseed I left by my flight tree. On the way across the field, I grab a handful and shove it in my pocket for later—in case the worms don't work out—and take three or four more handfuls and spread them across the ground.

Half the bag is gone before I get to the fence. I hide the rest of the birdseed under a pile of loose wooden posts and find a smashed straw hat with holes in it. The hat would look good on a scarecrow.

I choose a spot that's just to the side of the gate and twist one of the posts into the ground. Scarecrows are known to live up to their name. I'm hoping the one I'm building will be able to scare birds that get too close to the house, so Eleanor won't be able to catch them.

I find twigs and push them into the openings in the post for arms and legs and hang the hat at the top. It's not much of a scarecrow, but it will do for now.

In my room, I get my backpack ready for school. I make sure to grab the worms. I'm taking Teresa with me today too, just in case Eleanor comes in the room and searches for evidence while I'm at school. I know foster parents do that. They search for things, like notes or diaries, that can give them clues to who I am.

My white T-shirt is dirty. I choose my navy one to wear. I pull it over my head and sense without seeing her that Eleanor is standing in the doorway.

The people in my life who've seen the scar: Me. Some doctors, the EMT at Karen's. And now Eleanor.

She takes a deep breath. "You ready to go?"

I pull my shirt down fast. "It's not as bad as it looks." A version of a story about how I got it is probably in my file, but it doesn't tell the truth.

Eleanor folds her arms in front of her chest and shakes her head. "Looks like it hurt. I'm sorry." She sounds like she really means it.

"Why? You didn't do anything."

"I can still be sorry it happened to you, can't I?"

I give her one of my well-practiced shrugs as I pick up my backpack and book. The added weight of Teresa doesn't make that much difference, but I'm strong anyway. "I guess. It really didn't hurt that bad."

Even if it did, the scar is proof, proof of my wings.

9

Cheryllynn's not jumping rope this morning. There's no song to interrupt me from reading more about the red-tailed hawk. I take out the worm bag and open it all the way, sticking my fingers into the dirt to find a worm. I hold it up for inspection.

Scientists think raptors see eight to ten times better than humans. Their eyes are the largest organ relative to the size of their bodies. I don't have eyesight quite like that yet. If I did, I would've seen hot pink and lime green clothes coming my way.

The girls, the ones who called Cheryllynn by another name, look shiny and new. Everything from their hair to their clothes matches.

"What's that?" a few of them say.

They move like a murmuration, like how starlings twist and turn together in flight. Except, the flight patterns of starlings are beautiful, and these girls' unifying patterns have an ugliness to them.

"Is that a worm?" one of the girls says. "Were you about to eat it? That's so gross." She covers her mouth. "I think I'm going to throw up."

I drop the worm back into the bag. "No."

"Well, you looked like you were about to eat it. Do you eat them for breakfast? Do you save some for lunch?"

Another girl steps out of the group. "I think we should dare her to eat one right now." She grabs the bag out of my hand.

"Ew," the other girls say. They look really disgusted.

Maybe if I disgust them more they'll leave. "They're pretty good to eat actually. I bet none of you have tried a worm. You never know, you might like it."

Two of the girls are staring into my backpack now. One of them picks up my *Complete Guide to Birds: Volume One*.

I have to get their attention back to me. "I think *you* should eat one. Here." I grab for the bag of worms, but the girl holding it whisks it away.

"They're your worms," she says, and reaches into the dirt with pink-painted fingernails, finding a night crawler. "I dare you. I mean, you wouldn't have brought them if you weren't going to eat them, right?"

"Give her a break, Jenny. Maybe she needs extra protein," the girl with my bird book says. I'm not sure if she's being sarcastic or giving Jenny a solid reason why I have the worms.

"Matilda, don't tell me what to do." Jenny grabs my backpack.

"Why do you always pick on the new kids?" Matilda asks.

"I don't pick on them. I'm curious." Jenny reaches down into my backpack. "She brought worms to school."

She won't find *Bird Girl.* It's wrapped in my sweatshirt. It's safe. No one will find it. No one will read it.

"Oh, what is this?"

The group of girls leans forward in unison.

"What is it? Show us!"

Teresa is thrust into the air, looking out of place among all the bright colors, my sweatshirt caught on her talons. The sweatshirt falls to the ground before one of the girls catches her.

"It's a dead bird! An owl. Isn't it against the law to kill owls or something?"

The other girls, all except Matilda, chant, "*Hoo! Hoo!*" They don't sound like owls at all.

"Come on, the bell's going to ring." Jenny takes a step forward and holds the worm in front of me. "We don't have all day."

I can see the spine of *Bird Girl* exposed. The girls haven't spotted it yet. I need to grab it before they do.

"You can stand there all day. I'm not going to eat the worm."

My voice is quiet, raspy. It's getting ready to transform into an avian sound machine. Humans create sound using only two percent of the air exhaled through their larynx. Birds have what's called a syrinx instead. The syrinx is no bigger than an ant, but it's efficient and uses all the air that passes through it.

I don't have a syrinx, but I've been known to make annoying, wicked sounds. According to Karen, at least. I open my mouth, but no sound is there. I'm afraid. I'm afraid they're going to find my story.

Even if I had my wings, I wouldn't be able to fly away. My muscles twitch, but the rest of me is frozen like a potoo making itself look like a tree branch, trying its best to camouflage itself from the world. But there is no camouflage for me right now.

"Oh, but I think you *are* going to eat it." The girl pushes the worm close to my mouth. It squirms between her fingers.

Teresa flies over my head as the other girls start tossing her back and forth like a beach ball. She lands on the ground, right next to my sweatshirt.

"Hey, here's another book. It looks like a diary or something." *No!*

I run and try to grab *Bird Girl* out of the girl's hand, but she swipes it away before I can get to it.

"Let me see the book," Jenny says.

"I'll eat the worm!" I clear my throat and feel like I'm going to throw up. I can't let anyone, especially these girls, know what I really am.

"I'll eat the worm," I say again, "if you give me back that book."

"It definitely looks like a diary to me." Jenny flips through the pages, but doesn't stop long enough on any one to read the words.

Her friends are curious now.

"There's nothing in there"—I try to sound calm and cool—"it's just a book. My mom gave it to me." But then Jenny reads the title out loud. "If I eat one"—my voice isn't cool anymore—"will you give it back?"

Jenny holds her hand out so I can shake it. "Deal," she says, and hands me the worm.

I drop it in my mouth. I don't hold my nose. I don't squint my eyes in disgust. I stare right at the group of girls and chew, biting down hard to keep tears from falling. They have my book. They have my story.

I chew and chew until the worm is in parts small

enough for me to swallow. It doesn't taste good at all. As a matter of fact, it's disgusting.

I lean toward the girls and open my mouth. "See, it's gone. Now give me the book."

She shoves *Bird Girl* into a pink, sequin-covered purse. "No, I think I'm going to keep it for a while."

Some of the ways birds show anger: wing slaps, lunging, diving at intruders, sometimes colliding with other birds that invade their territory.

I want to run right at Jenny, but she'd just have to throw her purse to one of the other girls. "You don't even know me. Why are you treating me like this?"

"I saw you talking to Charlie yesterday," Jenny says, as if that explains anything. "We used to be friends. I'm actually doing you a favor. You're new here, so you don't know that he's not a good person to be friends with. I'm just trying to help you out."

"Why isn't she a good person to be friends with?" I don't know why Jenny keeps calling Cheryllynn Charlie. And Cheryllynn seems nice enough to me.

"Because."

" 'Because' is not really a reason, Jenny," Matilda says. I notice now she wears bright pink clothes, but her boots are cowboy, plain brown, a little scuffed at the toe.

Jenny gives her the evil eye to tell her to be quiet and

turns back to me. "So, here's my deal. If we see you hanging out or talking to him, you won't see your book again."

The girls leave Teresa and my bird guide on the ground. Walking away, they flock behind Jenny, following her like they're remote-control robots and Jenny controls the remote. Except for Matilda. She lingers behind the group, and I wonder if she's going to turn around, stay with me. But she still follows.

I taste dirt, and there are bits of sand in my teeth and on my tongue. It makes me gag. I bend over. Some birdseed from this morning sprinkles out of my pocket. I grit my teeth.

As soon as the girls are walking across the blacktop, I spit out as much of the worm taste as I can. I gag more, and on the second heave, throw up.

I can't help but stare at the small chunks of worm and the sunflower seeds I had this morning.

Bird Girl is mine. It's my story.

I have to get it back.

10

When we get inside the classroom, Mrs. Beck is playing music. It's low and soft, meant to inspire us to write. The music reminds me of thousands of leaves falling from trees.

The falling-leaves music is interrupted by the ring of the classroom telephone. Mrs. Beck answers. She hangs up the phone and heads straight toward me. She bends down. "December, the principal would like to see you. She wants you to bring your backpack."

When I get there, Cheryllynn is walking out of the nurse's office.

I look down, trying to pretend not to see her, hoping she won't notice me, either.

"Hey," she says. "You get in trouble?"

"Don't know." I keep staring at the floor.

Cheryllynn sits next to me. "I'll stay with you. I've been where you are before, waiting for the principal to talk to me. It's kind of scary."

I need to try and stay away from Cheryllynn, at least until I get my book back.

"So, you like birds, huh?" she asks.

Have Jenny and her friends already told everyone my secret?

"Why?"

"Well, the other day you were reading that book, and then you knew about black birds. I just put two and two together. Plus, I'm trying to keep your mind off having to see the principal." Cheryllynn pulls a bag of Froot Loops from a pocket of her pink raincoat.

"If you could, would you want to turn into one?" she asks. I wait for her to laugh a little, like her question is a joke, but she seems serious, like she wants to hear my answer.

"I mean, I think it would be cool to be an animal." Cheryllynn eats the pink pieces of cereal first. "I don't know if I'd want to be a bird, but a polar bear might be good, even though I don't think I'd want to get used to living in all that ice and snow, and I wouldn't like eating fish, or seals. They eat seals, right?"

I check the office to make sure Jenny or her friends aren't around. Sitting by the principal's office, weirdly, should be safe territory to talk to Cheryllynn. And anyway, everyone else is in class.

"But you'd be a polar bear, so it wouldn't matter," I say. "Snow, ice, and fish would be what you know, would just be how you lived."

"You're right." Cheryllynn picks out all the orange Froot Loops this time.

The principal's door opens. "Good morning, December." Mrs. Vaca holds her hand out for me to shake. "Please come into my office." She looks up at Cheryllynn. "Did you use the bathroom?"

"Of course I did," Cheryllynn says.

"Then you better get back to class."

"Is there something wrong with the regular bathrooms?" I ask Mrs. Vaca.

"No. There's nothing wrong with them." She sounds like she doesn't want to get into it. Cheryllynn stares hard at Mrs. Vaca but doesn't say anything. She waves as she heads back to class.

I don't wave back. I have to do whatever I can not to make her think we're becoming friends. Especially now.

The first thing I notice in Principal Vaca's office is the bright yellow umbrella leaning against the wall in a corner. Yellow would be too bright for my feathers. No matter where I go, I'll be able to hide with blue feathers, the color of the sky.

"December." Mrs. Vaca places her elbows on her desk.

"Another student has said you have something you're not supposed to bring to school. She said it might be dangerous. Can I see what you have?"

I zip my backpack open and show Mrs. Vaca Teresa. "It's just a stuffed bird. The only sharp thing it has on it is its talons. Owls needs sharp talons to catch food."

Mrs. Vaca sets Teresa on her desk.

"She's a great horned owl," I say.

"She's beautiful. I'm going to keep her here, and after school you can pick her up, okay?"

"Yeah." I stand up and start to leave.

Mrs. Vaca gently pats Teresa on the head. "The student who told me about you having this beautiful owl also claims you threatened to use the owl to hurt her. Is this true?"

"No." I grit my teeth again. Instead of clenching my fists, I tighten my fingers and spread them out like I have talons, like I am an owl, getting ready to catch prey.

Mrs. Vaca nods. "Okay, December." Her voice is a cool color, maybe turquoise, calm and steady. "That's all for now. Don't forget to come by after school and pick up your owl. And, please, do not bring her to school again."

When I start walking down the hallway, back to class, Cheryllynn is waiting for me.

"Everything okay?" she asks.

The part of the hallway where we walk is protected by

the outside walls of classrooms. But a few steps ahead, the classrooms stop and the hallway is open. If any girls were standing in the right place, they could see me talking to Cheryllynn.

"I'm fine." I walk faster, trying to lose her.

I turn the corner to the hallway where my classroom is, and just as I open the door and step inside, I hear Cheryllynn ask, "Why are you in such a hurry?"

During lunch in the cafeteria, I sit at the end of the farthest table from the door. I don't look up. I don't want to make eye contact with anyone. And at lunch recess, I hide behind the farthest tree on the playground.

After school, I hide, too, sinking down against the fence next to a planter where pink rosebushes grow.

A red car drives up to the curb. Jenny starts to get in, but before she closes the door, she looks toward the main entrance to the school and yells out, "Hey, Charlie, you need to tell your new friend to say she's sorry for trying to hurt me and my friends with her owl."

"The day you decide to live someplace far away is the day she'll apologize to you," I hear Cheryllynn say. "When are you moving?"

A faraway place would be Greenland. Jenny seems

like she'd be okay living on land that's mostly covered with ice. She'd have to learn to hunt for food, but she'd probably be a good hunter. She's definitely a good liar.

Jenny waves her hand like she's shooing Cheryllynn away and gets into her mom's car, but doesn't close the door.

I hear her mom. "I thought I told you to stay away from Charlie."

"I am," Jenny says.

"Well, I don't want you talking to him, either."

As her mom drives away, Jenny looks back and her eyes stay on Cheryllynn. It's not a mean stare. It's the kind of stare people have when they're daydreaming, or when they're remembering something, a memory of a place or of a person. Jenny said they used to be friends. Now they're not. It's not hard to figure out why.

But, when it comes to Jenny, the only thing I need to worry about is how to get my book back.

Cheryllynn leaves, too, the hood of her raincoat over her head. She kicks the ground as she walks. If I had *Bird Girl* in my possession, I'd kick the ground with her, and together our legs would have the power of a cassowary's kick, all the power we needed to keep people like Jenny away from us.

I don't believe kids are mean just to be mean. Most kids that are have a reason. Whether Jenny's reason is a good or bad one I don't know. But I do know that I don't like her. If Eleanor did ever stuff me, Jenny would probably think it was funny that I became just like Teresa.

Teresa! I forgot to pick her up. I run into the office and expect her to be sitting on the counter, but she's not there.

"December?" Mrs. Vaca says. "Your owl's in here."

Teresa's sitting on Mrs. Vaca's desk, and I pick her up, wanting to get back outside as fast as I can.

"Make sure you don't bring the owl back, December, okay?"

I stop inside the doorway, but don't turn around.

"Those claws could hurt someone," she says.

"Talons," I say. "They're talons. And I won't bring her anymore."

I wrap my arms around Teresa. My heart beats like a hummingbird's against her feathers.

I walk outside, and keep holding her as tight as I can.

11

Eleanor pulls up to the curb. I open the door, and she turns down the music. "How was your day?"

"I don't want to come back here." And I don't want to get used to Eleanor picking me up from school, or get used to her smelling like a mix of lavender and soil, or get used to her regular voice that really sounds like she wants to know how my day was.

"Why not?"

"Why are people so mean to each other?"

"Lots of reasons, I guess." Eleanor rests her hands on the steering wheel. "What happened today?"

I'm not going to tell her. I can't. What am I supposed to say, *There's this girl. She threatened to share my story, a story that tells the world I'm really a bird*? Eleanor would start making plans to stuff me.

I need to know more about Eleanor's "hobby." I ask,

"What are you going to do with Henrietta if she can't learn to fly?" I think I know the answer. "Are you going to stuff her?"

"No, December." Eleanor looks at me like she can see through to my feathers. "I'd never do that."

I'm not so sure I believe her.

The radio is turned off the rest of the way home. No singing. No music. When we get to the house, Eleanor says, "Come with me."

I follow her across the backyard, to the shed where I found Teresa. Eleanor turns on the light. The birds are dusty, making their feathers look faded. Behind me on the shelf is the red-tailed hawk.

Eleanor's voice is a soft shade of blue. "Over the years, I've found them in fields, or along the road. This might sound strange, but when I stuff them, I feel like I'm bringing them back to life in a way."

"You don't kill them just to stuff them, then?"

"No." Eleanor shakes her head. "Never."

"Here," she says, "I want to show you something else."

She sits down at a table. There are lots of lights, tools I don't know the names of, and a dead animal without eyes.

"Come a little closer and I'll show you what I'm doing." Eleanor slides on a pair of glasses. "You know what taxidermy is?"

"Stuffing dead animals." I lean over to get a closer look. A once-living thing with holes where its eyes should be is creepy. It would make a great scary movie, a bunch of about-to-be-stuffed animals coming alive, making the taxidermist so insane, she has no choice but to run away from her house. The stuffed animals end up catching the taxidermist anyway, and make her one of them.

Eleanor nods. "That's right. Do you know what kind of animal this is?"

"A weasel?" I guess.

"Close. A ferret. A neighbor's pet. Ferrets are known to be very smart animals. They can adapt quickly to anything life throws at them." Eleanor looks at me over her glasses and leans her shoulder close to mine, her voice a darker shade of blue. "I would imagine you can relate to that."

I shrug my shoulders. "Maybe. But it doesn't matter how well it adapts now; it's dead." I pet the top of the ferret's head with my finger.

Dead things don't bother me. Moving as much as I have, I've gotten used to things always changing. I've gotten used to things being there one day and being gone the next.

"He died from old age." Eleanor doesn't look up from the stiff animal. "His name was Frankie, and he was very much loved."

I touch Frankie's fur. "How can you grow a garden and stuff dead animals at the same time?" I ask. "That's a . . ." I can't think of the word.

"Contradiction?" Eleanor laughs, but not like she's making fun of me. "Well, I do this to make a little money on the side. Believe it or not, it pays for some groceries here and there. It's an art form, you know?" Eleanor picks up a bowl. "I mix up plaster to make a mold first. Then make a copy of the animal. It gives the animal a second life. In a symbolic way."

I understand what Eleanor means about "a second life." So far, I've found five orphaned dolls. I've come across them on the side of the road, in an almond orchard, and one hanging from a cyclone fence surrounding someone's front yard. Three have a missing arm or leg, one has a missing eye, and one doesn't have any hair. I keep them because someday I'm going to give them back what they've lost, even if I am a bird.

"Have you ever stuffed a macaw?" I ask.

"No. Macaws are beautiful birds, though."

"A stuffed one would make a good decoration, right?"

Eleanor places a small pair of scissors down on her work table. "Well, because they're beautiful, I suppose they would make a good decoration."

"But I wouldn't want to see a stuffed one, because they

are that beautiful. Did you know they live thirty to thirty-five years in the wild, but they can live eighty to a hundred years in captivity, if they're taken care of? Even though they live longer, I don't think something as beautiful as a macaw should spend its life in a cage. If it was me, I'd rather spend my life, even though it would be shorter, living where I was born to live."

"That's a good point." Eleanor smiles.

Her fingernails have dirt under them, and she squints her eyes like she's been looking at the sun all her life. Her smile is a good one. I have to remember not to get lost in it, though, or get lost in her being nice to me.

"I'm going to make dinner now," Eleanor says. Since I've been here, Eleanor's talked a lot about food. I thought she was trying to fatten me up, but maybe she just doesn't know what else to say. Or she's read that foster children are obsessed with where their next meal is coming from and she wants me not to have to worry.

Outside the shed, Eleanor stops. "Look." She points to three robins, perched on one of the bird feeders. "We'll see a lot of birds now. They'll be preparing for the coming of winter."

Even though Eleanor's told me about how she gets the birds she stuffs, I'm still going to be careful. I haven't lived with her long enough to hear all the calls of her bird whisper. Besides, even if I did know all her tones and cadences, my destiny is not with her. It's in the sky.

Walking behind Eleanor, I wave my arm in the air and scare away the three birds. "Migratory birds have to prepare more," I say. "Birds that were once just seed eaters will start eating worms and grubs. They need to store energy for the long flight ahead of them."

"If I were a bird, I don't think I'd be a migratory bird." Eleanor surveys the yard and stares up at the sky, waiting for the three birds to return. "I like to stay close to home."

"I'd definitely be a migratory bird."

"It would be more adventurous." Eleanor opens the door.

I pick up my backpack. "Is it okay if I go out again?"

"Stay close to the house, okay?"

"Don't worry, I won't get lost. I have good navigational skills. Like migratory birds."

Eleanor points to the sky. This time there's a red-tailed hawk circling high above the field. "Did you know the red-tailed hawk's scientific name is *Buteo jamaicensis*? *Buteo* is Latin and means *hawk*. *Jamaicensis* is named for Jamaica, the country, and from the Latin *ensis*, which means belonging to a place."

"I won't be out there for long. I promise." I don't wait

for her to say anything, and walk between the birdbaths, past the garden, and open the gate.

I'm not sure what "belonging to a place" means, and I'm not sure "belonging to a place" is the best thing. What Eleanor is talking about is having roots, a place to grow, but sometimes roots are pulled out. They get replaced with scars that cut deep, and either nothing can grow or what does grow is twisted and mixed up.

12

Out in the field, I look up through the branches of my flight tree. The best tier for Teresa would be the top one. It would give her the best view.

I start climbing, wind blowing through my T-shirt, blowing against my scar. The position of the branches makes it easy to move tier to tier, reaching up with my hands and pulling the rest of my body over the next branch.

I stop three tiers from the top and take off my backpack. The wind blows stronger up here and carries Eleanor's song from the kitchen, past the tree, and into the sky, where other birds will hear it. Hopefully, they will be too busy preparing for colder weather, and her song won't matter to them, like it can't matter to me.

I take Teresa out of my backpack and stand her up on the branch, leaning her against the trunk. She's at the mercy of gravity, just like me, and tumbles back into my arm.

I need something to secure her to the tree. I take off my socks and tie them together at the ends, tugging to make sure the knot is strong and tight. It's not the most liberating sight to see a stuffed owl tied to a tree trunk, but at least she's in her element, and that means something. Better than being in Eleanor's dusty taxidermy shed or sitting in a closet anyway.

I reach for *Bird Girl*, then remember it's gone. "They took my story," I whisper to Teresa. "I used to have wings, you know?"

Across the field, leaves fall from cottonwood trees, each one yellow and iridescent against the dimming light so that they look like miniature lanterns scattering over the ground.

I lie on the branch and find an open space to drop my backpack. I'm about fifteen feet from the ground.

I will fly.

This time I don't count. I don't take deep breaths. I don't wait to feel the scar on my back tingle. I just jump, focusing on keeping my body as streamlined as possible and positioning my arms and hands to maximize the catching of wind currents.

I hit the dirt. There is blood on my lip; I can taste it. I roll over on my back. The sky is light blue and yellow. I wonder a lot about where my mom could be. Does she think about me as much as I think about her? Does she sing "Happy Birthday" to me every December twenty-first? Does she wonder what I look like now? Would she be able to recognize me? Does she even have a place she lives, or has she turned into a migratory bird, too?

I've never called any foster place a "home." I've always called them "houses." A "home" is a place you feel you're supposed to be, where there are pictures on the wall of you when you were a baby, or on your first day of school.

I brush dirt off my pants and press the end of my T-shirt against my lip to wipe away any blood before walking into the house.

On the dinner table, Eleanor's set out a plate and a bag of sunflower seeds for me. She carries a bowl of soup across the kitchen and sets it down fast, spilling a little on the table. "Did you fall?"

I reach up and feel leaves that are caught in my hair. "Guess I did."

"There's dirt there, too." She points to my head, squinting her eyes to get a better look. "What happened?"

"I tripped. Over a root sticking out of the ground," I lie.

"You need to be careful when you're out there."

"I will." This isn't a lie. I do have to be more careful so I don't give away my secret.

She leans closer to me. "Doesn't look like you'll need any ice. Maybe a Band-Aid. I'll go get you one."

Eleanor keeps a first-aid kit in one of the drawers in the kitchen. She starts to unwrap a Band-Aid.

"I can do it," I say. "I'll do it."

"Okay." Eleanor gives me the Band-Aid, and I feel for where the scratch is.

Eleanor can't help watching. She must approve, because she picks up her spoon and starts eating her soup.

I crack a sunflower seed. "Can we go see Henrietta tomorrow?" I want to make sure I have enough time to get her to fly before my own wings unfold.

Eleanor smiles. "Absolutely."

"Last time we were there, I didn't see any other animals but Henrietta. You do help other types of animals, right?"

"We help any injured animal people bring to us, but mostly opossums, raccoons, and birds. Ninety percent of the animals that come to us we're able to set free." Eleanor spreads butter on some bread and dips it into the soup.

"What do you do with the other ten percent?"

"I've visited your school before." Eleanor doesn't answer my question. "I remember taking some hawks and other animals to share with the students. That's when I had Casey. I was able to train her to fly over the students, then fly back to me."

Maybe that's what Eleanor's planning to do, train me so even if I fly away, I'll always come back to her.

"She was a Cooper's hawk. I found her myself. She was caught in a barbed wire fence." Eleanor lifts her bowl, drinking the rest of her soup. "She knew I'd helped her, so she decided I was okay. Wild animals have a trust instinct, too. I provided her with food and a safe place to live. She could've flown away, but she kept coming back, and that was fine with me. I loved taking care of her."

"Why don't you still have her?" The question slips from my mouth before I can think about it.

"One day I took her outside, set her to flight, and she didn't come back. I guess she felt she was strong enough to be on her own. I believe she chose to leave, which was a good thing. She was a wild animal. Wild animals belong in the wild unless they have a wound that won't heal, an injury that makes it dangerous for them in their natural habitat. Most of the animals we get at the rehabilitation center are able to be reintroduced back into the wild. There's only a few we have to keep or find a new home for."

I crack a seed, trying not to make eye contact with Eleanor. All her talk of injured wild animals is making my muscles twitch.

"Have you ever brought home one of the animals that couldn't go back into the wild?"

Eleanor picks up her bowl and sets it on the counter by the sink. "Not home, but some do stay at the refuge. Sometimes, even when they're healthy enough to set free, there's a chance the animal won't make it in its natural habitat."

Eleanor is talking about me, that I might not be strong enough to make it out in the world by myself.

"This conversation is getting too serious." Eleanor wipes the counter with a dish towel. "Henrietta already trusts you enough to take food from you, so I think it'll be fine to start training tomorrow."

I don't know if any living thing has ever trusted me. People usually don't. I definitely know most of the time I don't trust people. I'm still suspicious of Eleanor, even though she's cleared up the whole taxidermy thing. Because if she really is the Bird Whisperer, she'll instinctually know what songs to sing to keep me in the nest. She'll know what migratory path I'll follow when it's time to find warmer weather. And she'll also know that whatever she does to make her home more comfortable won't do any good.

13

Behind the wildlife refuge is a field. At the edge closest to the building, there's a wooden perch.

"Okay," Eleanor says, "set her up there. What we're starting to do today is called 'creance training.' It's a form of exercise to build Henrietta's flight muscles."

Henrietta is perched on my hand. I thought I'd feel a little of her talons piercing through my skin, but the leather glove I wear is thick. She has anklets with long leather strips attached to them. The leather strips make a V shape and connect to a long string, which is connected to a longer rope that extends about thirty feet across to another perch.

"Let's try about halfway first." Eleanor is standing next to the far perch. "Don't worry if she flies to the ground. There's enough slack on the rope to give her the freedom to do that. If she does fly to the ground, go over and extend your glove. Hopefully, she'll hop back up and you'll be able to set her on the perch again."

I raise my arm so Henrietta can step onto the perch, and a bell attached to the glove rings a little. She doesn't want to go the first time. The second time, she steps onto the perch, but then flies to the ground, hopping around, tripping over the rope. She seems confused.

This isn't going to work.

But I follow Eleanor's directions and bend down and offer Henrietta my glove.

I swoop her up again. "I'm here for you," I tell her.

She clings to my glove with her talons and doesn't move. "I know you're scared, Henrietta, but if you want to fly again, we're going to have to build your muscles. It's like homework. I don't like doing homework, but all my teachers have said it's exercise for the brain. What you're doing is exercise. You want to get stronger, so you can go back to the wild where you belong."

Henrietta shifts her head side to side, like she's really thinking about what I just told her. This time, when I raise my arm to the perch, she steps up, steady, puffing out her chest a little.

Inside a pouch Eleanor gave me is a bag of raw meat. I walk to the halfway point between Henrietta and Eleanor, hold out my glove, and set a piece of the meat on top of it.

Henrietta doesn't move, but when I wave my glove up and down to ring the bell, telling her, "Fly!" she pushes off from the perch. She swoops low, then flies up and lands on my glove. She tears at the meat.

"Good job, Henrietta. That was amazing." Really, the amazing part is being able to see a bird like Henrietta fly so close to me.

"That was great, December," Eleanor says. "This time, take a few steps back and have Henrietta fly a little farther."

I don't know how long we're out here. I've lost track of time, but we don't stop until Henrietta has flown the whole distance, perch to perch, a couple of times. When we go back inside the refuge, I give Henrietta one last piece of meat, then place her in her cage. "If you keep flying like that, you'll be outta here in no time."

I stroke the top of her head with the tip of my finger and close the cage. I imagine Henrietta, a silhouette in the sky, circling for food, or perched on an electrical wire, watching the ground for a mouse, free to do what she was born to do.

Every living thing should have the freedom to be who or what they are.

As we're driving home, I ask Eleanor, "What'll happen to Henrietta if she isn't able to fly the way she needs to in order to survive on her own?"

"She'll stay at the refuge," she says.

So if I can't get Henrietta to fly, she'll live the rest of

her life in a cage. No bird, not even a flightless one, should have to spend its life trapped.

There was a story I heard from Wes. It was from a newspaper article. Thousands of blackbirds were found dead during the Fourth of July. People were setting off fireworks, and the sound and sparks scared the birds. They flew into telephone poles, cars, houses, and one another.

Those blackbirds were trapped by the sound of the fireworks, and they fell from the sky.

Tonight in my room, after Eleanor says good night to me, I think about Henrietta and how I need to practice so my flight muscles will get stronger, too. And I think of Teresa. She's keeping watch from the flight tree, her great horned owl family flying by to find out if the rumor that she's been brought back to life is true.

I peek down the hall to Eleanor's bedroom. The light is on. I'm patient, though, and wait till it turns off. Then I crawl to the living room, to my escape window.

It's cold. I don't feel it against my skin, but I see it in the moon and stars, bright and clear, looking like they've been carved and placed into the night sky.

I zigzag in and out of moonlight and look over my shoulder to Eleanor's house. Through the back fence, a porch light shines yellow, a slice of a miniature harvest moon, warm like the down comforter Eleanor gave me for my bed.

Tonight each branch on my flight tree can be seen in detail, and just like the moon and stars, they look like they've been placed with purpose.

The whole time I'm climbing, goose bumps form on my skin. The farther I climb the more I feel a cold wind blowing, just strong enough to make the leaves, still holding to branches, shudder. They move up and down, side to side, one falling, drifting down. That's not the way I've ever fallen. My falls have been hard, resulting in one sprained wrist and three sprained ankles. I'm not trying to hurt myself on purpose. I'm not. But it happens.

I'm trying to give my wings a chance. Getting hurt has nothing to do with it. I'd endure fifty thousand sprained ankles if it led to my wings unfolding again.

A teardrop falls on my arm, and I wipe my nose on my shirt. It's the cold making my eyes water. It's the cold making my nose run.

I climb to the branch where Teresa's perched. I stand up and shuffle my feet to the part where it's like a diving board, where I can feel it's flexible. I swear Teresa whispers, "Be careful."

"One, two, three," I whisper back. "Feathers will pop

through each goose bump." Real feathers, made from the protein keratin, the same substance that makes human hair.

I feel cartilage and bone tingle under my scars, but I think of the Latin name for red-tailed hawks, *Buteo jamaicensis*, and how Eleanor said *ensis* means belonging to a place.

As I stare down through branches tonight, the ground looks far away. My hands are sweaty. I let go with one and wipe the moisture off on my pants. My foot slips, and I hear my heartbeat, vibrating in the night, a *thump* against the cold. My heartbeat won't slow down. Either my wings are getting ready to burst from my skin or this is what being afraid feels like. I let go with my other hand, wipe it on my pants, and balance myself like birds naturally do, like I can naturally do.

Three is the magic number.

One. Eleanor must have other songs she sings. If I stay around, I'll get to hear them.

Two. There's Henrietta. She needs me now.

Three. I wonder how many dead birds' feathers it took to fill my comforter? It does keep me warm, but the warmth isn't worth the birds' sacrifice.

I will fly.

But I hesitate. The feel of falling will be nothing new. I'm used to it. The part I never get used to is hitting the ground. I never know if I'm going to land just right, without a scratch, or whether there will be a break.

Between the beats of my heart, a twig snaps on the ground, the sound coming from the direction of Eleanor's house.

"December?" I almost don't recognize Eleanor's voice. It's not her Bird Whisperer voice, it's more a mom-like sound, the tone of being afraid for a son or a daughter. Adrian sometimes has this tone when he talks to me, and I've heard it at school, too, when parents are picking up their kids.

Eleanor is wearing binoculars around her neck. She looks through them. It doesn't take long for her to find me. I hope she doesn't spot Teresa.

"There you are." She waves, letting the binoculars rest against her eyes. "The nights are getting cold. How long are you planning to stay up there?"

"You're not stopping me." My hands are holding tight to branches. I let go a little and feel my body lean forward. The skin over my scar is warm and getting warmer, the muscles, ligaments, bones beginning to twist into place.

"Stopping you from what?" Eleanor's feet tap against fallen leaves, each step a raindrop falling. "Just wanted to make sure you're okay. If you need food, I can bring it to you."

If her voice wasn't serious, I'd think she was teasing me.

"I can find food myself. And you don't have to take care of me."

"I want to take care of you. And Henrietta needs you. You were great together. If Henrietta keeps up what she did today, she'll be flying on her own in no time."

Eleanor stands to the side of the tree. "Oh, December, come down, please." Her Bird Whisperer voice is back. I wonder if the singsong rhythm is instinctual. Or maybe it's the voice she uses when she doesn't know what else to do. "Come down, December."

"If I don't, are you going to call the fire department?"

She doesn't answer. I hear Eleanor breathing, and something scraping against tree bark. She's climbing the tree.

"Just stay where you are." Eleanor is breathing hard. "Did you know there are birds that don't fly?"

I list three of them: "The emu, the emperor penguin, and the kiwi."

"Of course you would know that." Eleanor isn't even at the first tier and slips to the ground. She lands on her feet. "I can't do this," I hear her say. "December . . ."

"Kiwis are powerful little birds. They have strong legs so they can fight predators."

Eleanor looks up through the branches without using the binoculars. "Yes, they're birds that don't fly but are still amazing creatures. And, in my opinion, they're the smarter of birds because they stay on the ground."

"They can't fly," I say, "because that's how they evolved."

"True." Eleanor steps away from the tree, and this time uses the binoculars to look at me.

"Why'd you stop climbing?" I don't mean it to, but the question comes out angrier than it should. No one has ever climbed up after me.

"Well, to be honest, I'm afraid of heights," Eleanor says.

"Why?"

"I don't know. Just like it's not a matter of choice whether the kiwi flies, it's not my choice to be afraid of heights. I just am."

"You might be able to teach yourself how not to be," I say.

"Maybe." Eleanor lets go of the binoculars and rests her hands on her hips. "Have you ever heard of social weaver birds?" She's changing the subject. I guess she doesn't like to talk about what she's afraid of, either.

"I know they live in a colony, like one big family." I move down one tier. "They all share the same nest."

"Yes, their nests are believed to be the largest in the world. Some can get up to twenty feet wide and ten feet tall. Amazing. Most of the birds spend their lives maintaining the nests. Supposedly they do their job very well. Some nests have been known to last for almost a hundred years."

"That's a long time."

"Yes, it is."

"But a home is not always the best thing to have. Not all homes are happy, or safe."

"That's true." Even though Eleanor is on the ground, I still smell the lavender soap she uses. "But my home is safe. And I want you to stay for as long as . . ."

Eleanor stops talking. I wait for her to finish the sentence. *As long as* . . . I want. *As long as* . . . she'll have me. The truth is I can't leave now. I have to get my book back from Jenny. And I have to finish training Henrietta.

". . . I promise to be good to you," she says instead, "but you have to promise me something. If you want to come out to this tree—it's a beautiful tree—please ask. You can't leave and not let me know where you're going. At night, or during the day. I'm responsible for you. I take that responsibility seriously, whether you believe me or not. While you're here, I'll do whatever I can to help you, but you have to do your part. It's not a one-way street."

I lean forward a little. I squeeze the branch and catch myself, but for the first time since I started climbing trees, the feeling of falling scares me more than a little.

On the ground, where moonlight shines, Eleanor reaches up toward me. "December, please be careful."

I steady myself on the branch. "Don't worry," I say, "I'm okay."

But Eleanor's arms don't move. "I know I won't be able to stop you from climbing, but I want to know where you are, December. I want to know that you are okay. You might not think that's a big deal, to know where someone is, but it is to me."

I don't say, "I won't do it again," because I'm not sure I won't. I could lie, but not to Eleanor. I can at least give her that.

"Do you understand?" she asks.

I kind of believe Eleanor when she says, *I want to know that you are okay.* But I have to be careful.

I do understand what she's saying, but it's not going to stop me from trying to find my wings.

"You know what my favorite bird is?" Eleanor drops her arms.

There are ten thousand species of birds in the world, and even though I've never tried, I probably could come close to naming them all. "Well, from what I know about you, I'd say your favorite bird is the night parrot."

"Why the night parrot?"

"You seem like you want to hide from the world. You live way out in the country. Your house is hidden, too, with ivy growing all over it."

"Well, I do like living out here, but not because I'm trying to hide from the world." Eleanor steps out of the moonlight, so now she's just a voice I hear from the ground. "No, swallows are my favorite. They're everyday birds. I love seeing them fly out from under bridges, or swoop close to the river's surface to get a drink of water. I like how they're not territorial, but they'll fiercely defend their nests if needed."

It's quiet. I wait for Eleanor to keep telling me about swallows, or to ask what my favorite bird is, but there's no sound. Grabbing branches, I move down one tier. I can't see Eleanor from here, either.

"Eleanor?"

"Yes, I'm here. I'm ready to go back inside. What about you?"

"Maybe."

"I'd like you to come down. By the way, I make really good pancakes for breakfast." Eleanor holds the binoculars against her eyes again. "And I have plenty of butter and syrup."

Pancakes with lots of butter and syrup would be a nice way to store energy for my journey ahead.

14

On Monday, I stand on the edge of the playground, looking for Cheryllynn to make sure I go in the opposite direction. There's a strip of fog floating over the grass; the kids out in the field run in and out of the heavy moisture, turning into ghosts.

I find a tree with leaves that look like giants' hands and lean against the trunk, holding my backpack against my chest this time.

I need to figure out how I'm going to get *Bird Girl* back. I could just walk right up to Jenny, grab her purse, and run. I could pick a fight with her. I'm pretty sure I could wrestle her to the ground and pin her nose to the dirt until she gave me back my story.

There's only one problem with these plans: I'd be the one to get in trouble. I'd be the one accused of stealing, or bullying, even though it was Jenny's fault. Jenny who stole from me.

Through the fog comes a song. Across the playground, Cheryllynn is singing a jump rope rhyme: *"Cinderella, dressed in blue, who's gonna go to the ball with you? A, B, C . . ."*

It doesn't take long for Jenny and her friends to find Cheryllynn. They gather around her and start doing what they seem to do best, act like vultures.

"Where'd your mom get that raincoat anyway? Did she find it on the street?" The girls' voices are what I think guinea fowls sound like, annoying and screechy.

I don't know why they're always teasing Cheryllynn about her raincoat. It's pink. It's bright. It's shiny. Everything they seem to like. They're just jealous.

"It's not even raining." Jenny's pink sequin purse is hanging from her shoulder, but she might've taken *Bird Girl* and hidden it somewhere else.

As far as I can tell, the object of Jenny's game is to see if she and her friends can peck at Cheryllynn until she disappears. I'm going to call the girls "the Vultures."

Cheryllynn keeps jumping rope, humming another rhyme.

Vultures have a keen sense of smell. That's how they find carrion—dead and decaying meat of animals. And that's how the Vultures see Cheryllynn. The way they see me. They like to peck and tear.

They form a circle around her. "Why'd you pick that name anyway? Tell us, you really did get that raincoat from the lost and found, right?"

"Aren't you going to answer our questions?" The Vultures try to move in front of each other, like scavenger birds hissing for a better spot to feed.

"No." Cheryllynn stops jumping. "Because Jenny could tell you where I got it."

Jenny steps forward, closer, joining Cheryllynn inside the circle. "I saw her take it out of the lost and found."

"Try again," Cheryllynn says. "You were with your mom when you saw me buying this coat and the boots to match. You seemed like you were almost going to wave hi to me. You know, we used to say hi to each other all the time. But then your mom saw me, too, and told you to 'come on.'"

"We used to say hi to each other before you forgot that you're really a boy."

"No, we used to say hi before your mom and dad said they didn't want you hanging around with me anymore."

"Wrong. That's not what happened. You decided you didn't want to be friends anymore. You made your choice."

"You can tell whatever story you want." Cheryllynn stares right at Jenny. "I know the truth."

"Well, it doesn't matter really. My mom and dad are right. I shouldn't hang out with you."

Cheryllynn kicks the grass with the tip of her boot, turns around, whisks her hood off, and pulls a hair tie from her hair. The strands of her hair are frizzy, standing up in all directions, like tree branches spreading toward the sky. "You know what matters? I'm exactly who I'm supposed to be."

Jenny steps back into her space of the circle that surrounds Cheryllynn. "I didn't see you at a store buying that coat. I saw you take it from the lost and found. That's the truth."

"That's a lie," Cheryllynn says.

As I turn around, I bump shoulders with Matilda. I glare at her and keep moving.

"I'm sorry. I'm not like them, you know?" she says. "I came to this school right before you did. I'm new, too. Jenny was nice to me, so . . ."

"So . . . ," I say over my shoulder.

"She's someone to hang out with."

"I wouldn't hang out with her in a hundred fifty million years."

As I walk across the blacktop, I look over my shoulder. Matilda stares at Jenny, at the group, at Cheryllynn. Cheryllynn's not surrounded by the circle anymore. She's made her way in front of the girls, hands on her hips. She's not backing down from them.

I have to get *Bird Girl* back. There aren't many choices I have in my life, but what I do with my story is one.

No matter where I go on the playground, I can hear the echo of the Vultures' voices. They don't stop till the bell rings, leaving Cheryllynn alone, a faded pink dot in the middle of the grass.

I should've stayed with her. I wouldn't have had to say anything. I could've just stood next to her, to show her I was there.

Some birds are more loyal to each other, like storks, geese, and swans. They've been known to stay together during migration when they're traveling hundreds of miles.

I wish I could've been a goose for Cheryllynn.

After school, Eleanor honks the horn and waves. Soon as I get into the truck, it starts to rain. As we're driving down the road, windshield wipers squeak. Out the window, through raindrops, a blurry pink figure appears. It's Cheryllynn. I think about Jenny's deal, and look in the side mirror to see if her mom's car is behind us. "Can you stop the truck? That's a girl I know, Cheryllynn."

Eleanor pulls over, and I open the door. "Want a ride?" I say it so quiet, Cheryllynn doesn't hear me.

"Would you like a ride home?" This time she does. She looks up at me, but doesn't move toward the truck.

"It's not that far of a walk," she says. I don't blame her for not wanting a ride from us, from me.

"Maybe not . . ." I scoot across the seat. "We still can give you a ride."

She plops inside the truck, drops of rain falling from the ends of her hair.

"You're Cheryllynn?" Eleanor says. "Nice to meet you."

"Nice to meet you."

Eleanor shakes Cheryllynn's hand. "Where are we taking you?"

"Just to Sav-Mor Market. My mom works there."

Eleanor turns down the music. "How long have you lived here?"

"Since I was in second grade," Cheryllynn says.

"You like it?" I ask.

"Yeah, but I'd be okay living anywhere with my mom, you know?"

I kind of know what Cheryllynn means. I think I could live anywhere with Eleanor, whether it was the coldest place on earth, Oymyakon, Russia, which recorded a temperature of ninety degrees below zero, or the hottest place on earth, Death Valley, where scientists have recorded the temperature at one hundred thirty-four degrees. As long as there was a chance to fly, I'd be okay.

Sav-Mor Market is at the end of the block. Eleanor parks in front.

Before Cheryllynn gets out of the truck, she asks, "Want to come in and have a slushy?"

Eleanor follows behind us, and as Cheryllynn opens the swinging door to the store, she starts chattering again. "My mom will probably tell you this when you meet her, but call her Rhonda. She doesn't like to be called Mrs. Watts by anyone who's friends with me."

Rhonda stands behind one of two cash registers. Her hair is cut really short. She wears lots of makeup—pink eye shadow and red, red lipstick. Long peace-sign earrings dangle from her ears. Soon as she sees Cheryllynn she gives her a hug. "How was your day?"

"Good." Cheryllynn points back at me. "This is December, and her mom, Eleanor."

I don't correct Cheryllynn about Eleanor being my mom. She is, for now.

Rhonda reaches her hand out for me to shake. "Hello. Nice to meet you."

I hesitate, then put my hand in hers. It's warm, and soft.

She turns to Eleanor and shakes her hand, too. "Good to meet you. If you two want a slushy, help yourselves."

Cheryllynn pulls me down the aisle. There are two flavors, cherry and blueberry. "I like to mix them," she says, pressing down on a lever.

I fill my cup with cherry and follow Cheryllynn to aisle eight. There's a section that's a paradise of plastic toys.

Cheryllynn picks up a wand and twirls it around. "Abracadabra, I turn you into a . . . What do you want to be?"

"A bird, please," I tell her.

"What kind?"

"I'd like the hummingbird's acrobatic ability, the gentoo penguin's skills as a great swimmer, and the albatross's ability to fly long distances."

Cheryllynn twirls the wand around again. "Abracadabra, I turn you into all the birds you just said. I can't remember them all. How do you remember all those things about birds?"

"It's just easy for me. Things about birds stick in my brain. I was born with a bird brain, you know?"

Cheryllynn spits red slushy back into her cup and laughs. I laugh, too. It's a strange sound, only because I haven't heard it much. The sound keeps going and going, evolving into one I've never heard at all, a laugh that makes its way down into my stomach and shakes my whole body. I can't stop.

We're like a flock of nightingales singing.

All the laughing has made me forget about Jenny. I can't make her mad. Maybe she comes to this store. Maybe she's in the next aisle, listening to Cheryllynn and me.

"I think I should go," I say, but Cheryllynn is holding the wand out for me to take.

I don't grab it right away. "Just a second." I check aisle seven and aisle six. No Jenny. No Vultures.

"You okay?" Cheryllynn asks as I take the wand.

"Turn you into a princess, right?"

"Of course, and don't hold anything back. I want to wear everything a princess should wear, a gown, tiara, high-heeled shoes." Cheryllynn holds her arms out to the side and closes her eyes. I wonder if she believes when she opens them, she'll really be a princess. "Everything pink, even the diamonds."

"Abracadabra. I turn you into a princess." I wave the wand and point it at Cheryllynn.

She opens her eyes and looks down at her clothes. "That trick never works, but it's always fun to try. You know, the first day I wanted to wear a dress to school, my mom said no. Not because she didn't want me to be who I wanted to be, but because she was afraid kids would make fun of me, and that I'd get beat up. She was trying to protect me."

"You probably went to school wearing a dress anyway, right?"

"No. That day my mom said I should try wearing just a bracelet and a ring at first and see how that would go. I didn't care what anyone thought, but I guess she was afraid. Little by little we added more things until a dress—it was actually a skirt—wasn't a shock."

I lift the wand. "Want me to try again?"

"No," Cheryllynn says, "I'm good."

Wandering the aisle, I don't get any farther than the butterfly wings hanging inside plastic bags. At first I just stare at them, but I can't help myself, and open one. I just want to see how they feel, even though I know my real wings will feel a lot different. I thread my arms through the straps. If Jenny came around the corner right now, I doubt the wings would cause her to mistake me for a butterfly. But still. It's nice, for a second, to look over my shoulder and see them.

"Those look good on you. Like you were born to wear them," Cheryllynn says. "I could buy them for you, if you want." She grabs the wings. "The blue ones, right?"

"No. I don't need them."

"You sure?"

"I'm sure. Thanks, though. I don't think I deserve them. I saw Jenny . . ."

"I saw you walk away."

"Yeah, I did." I grab the wings back from Cheryllynn and hang them on the hook. "I shouldn't have, but Jenny took something that belongs to me. She'll only give it back if I don't hang out with you."

Cheryllynn takes a sip of her slushy. "You know, Jenny and I used to be really good friends. Best friends, actually."

"That's hard to believe."

"When I started wearing dresses to school, her parents didn't want her hanging out with me anymore. All the teasing is her way of getting back at me. She believes it's all my fault that we're not friends. That's the story she has to tell herself. But she made a choice. And I did, too."

"I'm sorry," I say. I made a choice, too, and it was the wrong one.

Eleanor and I say goodbye. As we walk out of the store, I scan the parking spaces. There isn't any car that looks like Jenny's mom's.

Inside the truck, looking down at red ice in my cup, warm air blowing against my skin, I stare at Eleanor's hands. Bluish-green veins rise up from her skin, like a map of rivers, one branching out from another. I want to reach over and press one. The skin looks soft and squishy.

"Cheryllynn and her mom are nice," Eleanor says. "Maybe we can invite them to dinner sometime?" I bet her veins are like the Mississippi River. Her heart is so big, she has deep, wide veins to handle the blood needed to keep it beating.

"That would be okay." Seeing Cheryllynn and her mom together, the way they treat each other, gives me hope.

But hope is a scary thing.

Maybe I'm not a bird. Maybe I'm not even part bird. Maybe I'm just an eleven-year-old girl with a scar on her back where wings will never unfold, no matter how hard I try to make them.

I look down. My arms have goose bumps even though heat's blowing through vents, and Eleanor's singing, bringing her own warmth, too. But the goose bumps aren't there because I'm cold. They're there as a reminder. *You are a bird, and goose bumps are where each feather belongs: layered, beautiful, strong.*

15

Today, when I stick the glove into Henrietta's cage, she ruffles her feathers and hops back, like she's afraid of me.

"It's okay," I whisper, and give her a piece of raw meat.

As we're walking out to the field, Henrietta moves back and forth across my glove, spreading her wings a couple of times. "She's not herself," I tell Eleanor. "I think she's afraid of something. Me, maybe?"

"No," Eleanor says. "She's just familiar with the routine now. Knows what to expect. Kind of like an athlete right before a big race." She looks up at Henrietta, standing on the perch. "We'll keep coming out here as long as it takes. There's no need to set a world record for flight today."

I take my position in the field, next to a perch, about ten feet farther than last time. I wave my glove up and down, jiggling the bell. Henrietta doesn't move.

"Try again," Eleanor says.

I do, but Henrietta doesn't take flight. "What if I move closer?"

Eleanor nods. "Let's try it."

I move to a spot closer than I was the first time we were out here and jiggle the bell, and this time Henrietta flies to me.

But during the rest of our training session, Henrietta refuses to fly any farther.

On the way home, I ask Eleanor, "Did I do something wrong? If she keeps doing this, she's never going to fly."

"She just regressed a little. We have to keep being there for her. She'll come around. Don't worry. You'll get her to fly."

I'm not so sure. Maybe I'm not the right person to teach her, after all. Maybe Henrietta, with her keen bird sense, has decided not to give me her trust. She knows that things don't usually work out for me.

"Don't worry, December," Eleanor says again. "Hey, Halloween is coming up. Should we go get some pumpkins? What do you think?"

Eleanor is trying to get my mind off Henrietta. I don't know if it'll work, but I like that she's making an effort.

"That would be good."

Eleanor turns down a dirt driveway that leads to a pumpkin patch.

Orange. It's everywhere. But pumpkins are the best of what orange can be: pumpkins, Popsicles, and sunset skies.

Eleanor wanders the patch, searching for a pumpkin. When I catch up to her she asks, "Have you found one you like?"

"You want me to pick out a pumpkin?"

"Don't you want to?"

"I guess. What are you supposed to look for in a good pumpkin?"

Eleanor rests her hands on her hips. "I've never been asked that question before. I don't really know. You just pick ones that you like." She points to a patch of light blue pumpkins that break up the orange. "Those are Cinderella pumpkins. The green ones are called Fairytales. Then, you have Big Rocks, which are good for carving jack-o'-lanterns, and over there"—Eleanor turns around—"the big white ones are Full Moon pumpkins."

"I like the orange, regular ones." It doesn't take me long to pick out three, and Eleanor and I take them to the truck.

"They have a corn maze, too," Eleanor says. "You want to walk through it?"

One thing I've noticed about Eleanor is she's always asking me whether I want to do something or not. She's giving me choices.

The path we're supposed to take is clear, and not too confusing, but it feels like the maze goes on a long time. I start to wonder if it has an end. We turn—and suddenly I've lost track of direction.

"Think we're almost there." But we turn the corner and the path continues.

The cornstalks have become an endless wall. I take deep breaths, my oxygen and carbon dioxide exchange getting faster and faster, and I think about Jenny. She still has my book. She has my story, and the secrets it tells of my bird self. Stories and secrets that are only mine to share. My heart beats like a hummingbird's now.

"December." Eleanor rests her hands on my shoulder. I jump a little even though her touch is still featherlight. She sings softly.

My breathing slows, and I hear Eleanor's voice saying, "We're okay. We'll find our way out. Together. I'm not going anywhere. I promise."

She holds out her hand for me to grab, but I'm not ready to take it. We walk side by side, though, and in four turns, we've made it to the end.

Back in the car, it feels good to sit in the truck with the heat coming through the vents. My feathers, my dormant feathers, are not bothered by the air right now.

"I get nervous." I hold one of the pumpkins in my lap.

"Sometimes . . . I get nervous when I think I can't get out of a place. I don't like spaces that make me feel that way."

Eleanor leans over the steering wheel, her voice a dusky blue. "When I was growing up," she says, "I was afraid of the dark. Like really afraid. I slept with the light on until I was a teenager. But now, one of my favorite things to do is to go outside at night and just sit. Sit with the noises, even if it's quiet. That's what scared me most about the dark. I was always thinking about what noises I'd hear at any minute. It caused me a lot of anxiety."

"So I'll get over it someday?"

"More than likely you'll grow out of it." Eleanor pats the pumpkin. "You ready to go home?"

Home. I don't want the word to make me feel the way I did the first time I saw a blue heron take flight. As soon as its feet left the earth, the ground shook a little, and my breath was taken away. Seeing the blue heron made me feel like everything was connected, and that, like Adrian's told me a million times, the world and I were going to be okay. Most people would want to feel that way, but I can't. If I feel too okay, I'll lose the desire to find my wings.

In the driveway, Eleanor turns off the ignition. "I want you to know, I'm here for you, December."

"But not for long. You're a foster parent, which means your house is temporary."

Eleanor leans over the seat. Behind me, in the field, there's another oak tree, but it's a valley oak, shorter, stockier than my flight tree. Eleanor's eyes rest on the spot where it grows. I wonder if she's thinking about the word *temporary*.

"I don't have to be," she says.

"What do you mean by that?"

"I mean you can stay with me for as long as you want. What do you think of that?"

"Maybe" is all I can say to that right now. Because staying with Eleanor would not be a realistic life for a bird.

I get out of the truck, carrying the pumpkin that I was holding in my lap, and set it on the porch. I do the same with the other two pumpkins.

I open the side gate and go into the backyard, heading to my flight tree. I see three broken birdhouses are on a table. One needs half its roof replaced. I stand over it. Inside is just one room, no windows except for a small round one next to a perching post.

"After these birdhouses are fixed, we can build something together, if you want?" Eleanor stands inside the back door, the screen fading her into a shadow.

I don't remember ever building anything with my mom, not even a puzzle or anything with blocks.

"What would we build?"

Her silhouette says, "A desk for your room? A chair

to go with the desk? Anything you want. You could paint it any color, too."

"I don't really need anything, though."

"Well, maybe you can think about it."

The screen door clicks shut. Eleanor goes back to the kitchen.

I want to try to fix the roof on the birdhouse. All the tools I need are here: measuring tape, a small handsaw, hammer, and nails.

If people could fix memories like they fix a house, covering up holes, stopping leaks, hanging doors back on hinges, then bad images couldn't get through.

As I'm fitting the cut pieces of wood to the roof, five birds gather on the ground under one of the bird feeders. They're pecking at the dirt where seeds have fallen down.

Bluebirds' wings are not really blue. The blue is caused by light waves interacting with each feather. The colors bouncing back to the human eye are in the blue range. When my feathers appear, what Eleanor will see is just blue, and she will be so mesmerized, she won't care I'm flying away because something as beautiful as me should be free.

At dinner, Eleanor eats leftover soup. There are bread rolls in a basket covered with a red-and-white-checkered towel, and the butter is in a dish in front of me. Eleanor grabs a roll, cradling it in her hands. "Warm." She pulls it apart and spreads butter on each side of the roll.

She offers me the bread basket.

The bread and the butter smell good. I don't want to get too used to good things, but I also need to store fat for my journey ahead. I take a piece of bread, tear it, and spread a glob of butter on each half.

"You want to carve the pumpkins after we eat?" Eleanor dips the bread in the soup and takes a bite.

"I'm kind of tired."

"Tomorrow, then."

After we finish washing dishes, I go to my room and find my blue leggings and blue tank top. I have to dress light.

To create lift, a force has to equal or exceed gravity, which means I need to jump hard into the air. I also need my wings to be as smooth as possible to reduce drag. I don't weigh much, but I still need to be balanced. Thrust will be the hardest. If my wings unfold, they need to be strong enough to sustain acceleration.

I wait till Eleanor checks on me, popping her head into my room and whispering, "Good night."

"Good night," I say. I like Eleanor. I do. She's nice. I believe she really does care about me, even though if she had a chance, like if suddenly I died and they did an autopsy and found wings embedded under my skin and bone, she might think, *What an amazing specimen. I must stuff and keep her forever.* I wouldn't even blame her for feeling this way. I'd want to keep me, too.

But I can't let myself feel too much of anything for Eleanor. She asked me what I thought about staying with her. My answer is, my time here is now defined by how long it will take Henrietta to fly, which might not ever happen. It's also defined by how long it will be before my wings unfold.

I tiptoe down the hallway, checking the living room. The front door is the easy exit, but it squeaks. I hear Eleanor snoring, but I don't want to take the chance of waking her up.

The clock on the stove reads 10:16. I use the back door. Before taking a step outside, I listen to the sound. I swear she's snoring the "Eleanor Rigby" song. Against my cheek I feel the warmth of the house, and take a deep breath of the air, which smells like bread, butter, and lavender. I close the door.

Moonlight shines on the rows of vegetables. What Eleanor created is beautiful. But beyond the garden are shadows of trees, bare branches reaching out to me, waving for me to come join them. The muscles between my shoulder blades twitch and tingle. Muscles have memory. My muscles have memory of flight.

Birds have an amazing homing sense. They can navigate their way from nesting place to nesting place even if knocked off course. The arctic tern makes the longest annual migration; it travels thousands of miles, zigzagging between Greenland and Antarctica. In its lifetime the arctic tern is known to make the journey around thirty times. That means in its lifetime it migrates one and a half million miles. That's three trips to the moon and back.

Scientists don't exactly know why birds can navigate so well, but they think it has something to do with having magnetite in their beaks. Some birds use landscapes to find their way, and some learn migration routes from their bird parents.

Homing is an animal's ability to return to a place or territory after having traveled a great distance from it. In my case, there haven't been a whole lot of places or territories I want to return to. Not yet. Within the word *homing* is the word *home*. In my file, it would also say, *December has no real understanding of what a home is. She hasn't had time to really define what it means to her. In her case, it's understandable that she has a tendency to not want to stay in one place.*

There's a layer of fog above the field. Everything

is faded, has no color, the closest the world gets to black-and-white.

In the dark, I feel goose bumps on my skin. *They're not goose bumps,* I remind myself. *They're your body's way of getting ready for wings.*

I will fly.

Climbing the tree, I feel my foot slip. I slide it back, press into the branch, and steady myself. I take a deep breath to slow down my heartbeat. This time I don't count before I jump, but right before my feet leave the branch, I wish I was back in my room, and as I'm falling I see the bread and butter sitting on Eleanor's table, and hear her say, *You can stay with me for as long as you want.*

When I hit the ground, my ankle twists under my weight. I crawl, and sit against the trunk of the tree. Pain throbs in rhythm with my heart, beating slower now, a normal, human, nothing-special sound.

I limp toward the house. My ankle hurts. A lot. As I open the gate, the back door closes. Eleanor stands with her arms folded in front of her, giving me a raptor-like glare. "You can't do that anymore, December," she says. "You can't sneak out. Not in my house. Not for as long as you're with me. I will take care of you. I will be kind to you, but you can't just take off any time you want."

I don't want her to notice that I'm limping, so I stand

like a heron, waiting for a fish to catch. "I'm sorry." I can't remember the last time I was the one apologizing. Usually people say it to me. Adrian says it all the time.

"You have good balance. Why are you standing like a flamingo?"

"Thought I looked more like a blue heron."

"Well . . ." Eleanor bends down to get a closer look at the ankle I'm holding up. "According to scientists they both stand on one leg for the same reason. But I don't think you're trying to conserve body heat right now."

Eleanor barely touches my ankle, and it hurts. "Let's put some ice on that."

She leans forward and scoops her arm across my scar. I let myself lean against her. "I hurt my ankle," I tell her, even though she's figured that out already. What she doesn't know is I've never said the words "I hurt," either. Not to Adrian. Not to anyone.

16

Before going to school, Eleanor and I drive to the wildlife refuge, and I exercise Henrietta.

At the edge of the field there's the spicy smell of leaves, and the ground's covered with shades of brown and yellow.

"We're going to take it slow today. We'll start off with a short distance again." Eleanor moves one of the perches out into the field.

Henrietta's walking back and forth on my glove, acting like she did the other day. When I hold her up so she can hop on the perch, she spreads her wings and flutters to the ground.

"It's okay," Eleanor says, but Henrietta, hopping on the ground, looks like a broken bird.

"Go to her." Eleanor waves her hand. "Place your glove down close to her so she can hop up. Try to get her on the perch again. You can do this, December."

I follow Eleanor's directions. Henrietta hops away from me, but I gently crouch close to the ground and hold out my glove until she hops onto it.

Soon as I walk out to the perch, I tell Eleanor, "I don't think she wants to be out here."

Eleanor, being Eleanor, says, "It's okay. Henrietta will be okay. Be patient. Give her time."

But I'm right. Henrietta won't budge from the perch.

"I told you, Eleanor." I take off my glove and give it to her. "Maybe she'll trust somebody else."

On the way to school, Eleanor tries to convince me that Henrietta will be fine. "She'll come out of it. We'll get her up and flying. Sometimes the only thing you can do is to keep trying. I know that's not as exciting as seeing a majestic bird like Henrietta fly, but, unfortunately, that's all we can do right now."

Before I shut the truck door, Eleanor gives me a smile that I can tell she wants to mean *everything is going to be okay* and says, "Henrietta is going to fly, December."

Eleanor is probably right, Henrietta will fly, but I'm not the right person to get her to. She doesn't trust me after all. I'm not the one who's going to help her.

I throw my backpack by my classroom door.

At the edge of the blacktop, the Vultures are gathered in a group like they always are, pecking and tearing at Cheryllynn. I move around the basketball court and get close enough to hear what they're saying.

"Your hair," Jenny says. "It's too long, don't you think?"

"No," Cheryllynn says, "I don't think it's long enough."

"Cheryllynn?" I say. My voice is shaky. I could stop right now and turn around, but I think of Henrietta and the image of her fluttering to the ground. I can't help her, but maybe I can at least help Cheryllynn. "You want to jump rope with me?"

Before Cheryllynn can answer, Jenny struts up to me. She holds up the pink sequin purse in front of her. "Did you forget I have this?"

"Yeah," Cheryllynn says. "Yeah, I'll go jump rope with you."

She pushes past Jenny and stands shoulder to shoulder with me.

"You are not going to jump rope with her." Jenny unzips her pink sequin purse. She opens *Bird Girl*, runs over by the play dome, and steps up onto the lower bars.

"Good morning, Fairview Elementary! I have something to share with you. This is December's book. She doesn't want anyone to read it, but I think it's important we get to know the kind of person she is."

Jenny starts to read. Her voice is the brightest shade of orange there is, and mixed with the orange is yelling. She wants the whole school to hear her. *"My mom took me out to the orchard, so I could fly."*

The three-wattled bellbird has one of the loudest bird-calls on earth. My call is more like a crow's, a normal, everyday *caw, caw,* but I make it sound as fierce as I can.

I run past the Vultures, my T-shirt flapping in the wind. Jenny stops reading. The whole playground is quiet. If they have any interest in birds, they might be trying to identify what species I am, and come to the conclusion there's no other bird like me. Or they're telling themselves, *That's that girl, December. She's strange. During recess she sits under trees. Hangs out by herself.*

That's not what I care about, though. I care about protecting my story.

I hop up three rungs, pull myself through an opening, and perch my blue high-tops at the edge of the monkey bars.

"Young lady, get down off there," a yard duty lady yells. "Young lady!"

I straddle the bars, balancing myself without using my arms. The bars are still wet, the wind strong, cold, blowing my hair back so the brown strands look like a cape, or even better, a layer of feathers.

Jenny flips through the pages. *"December did fly, but she only flew from walnut tree to walnut tree.* This is so weird. She thinks she can fly?"

One of the Vultures starts chanting, "Jump! Jump! Jump!" The rest of the girls follow. Matilda, wearing her brown boots, waves her arms in front of them and yells, "You guys need to stop! Be quiet!" But the Vultures don't listen.

Jenny keeps reading. *"December's wings are . . ."*

Before Jenny can read the rest of the sentence, Cheryllynn comes up from behind her, jumps up, and grabs the book. "That's December's!"

Jenny slips off the bars of the play dome, but hangs on to the book. There's a tug-of-war between her and Cheryllynn. If the other girls help Jenny, it'll be all over.

I have to keep their attention. I move my right foot in front of my left and start walking along the edge of the bars, this time using my arms for balance. I tuck my chin to my chest and fall forward. I flip through the air, and I'm sure I hear some of the Vultures gasp.

I miss the landing, slipping on the wood chips. There's a little blue between the fog, and then there's Cheryllynn, leaning over me. "If it wasn't for the wood chips you definitely would've nailed the landing," she whispers. "That was amazing. You're rock star material."

She offers her hand to pull me up, and I take it.

"Think this belongs to you." Cheryllynn gives me *Bird Girl*. "Thanks for standing up for me."

I cradle my story. "Thanks for getting this back. It means a lot to me."

A yard duty lady comes up to us. "You can't be jumping off the play equipment. I'm going to have to send you to Mrs. Vaca." She gives me an office slip.

I don't care if I have to go to the principal's office. I have *Bird Girl* now. I look over my shoulder. Jenny and the Vultures are huddled in their group like nothing even happened.

A long time ago, when I was six years old, I used to think I'd like having a friend named "July" because July out of all the months is the opposite of December. July would wear pretty dresses and sparkly shoes and smell like bubble gum all the time.

Cheryllynn, who volunteered to come with me to the office, wears Halloween black tights, black boots, and a bright lime green jacket. She doesn't smell like bubble gum, but she does smell like Froot Loops.

"You're limping," Cheryllynn says. She offers me some cereal.

I'd forgotten all about my injured ankle. Now that I remember I hurt it, I feel it throbbing. "I'll be okay," I tell her, and I shove *Bird Girl* down inside my backpack.

Mrs. Vaca is waiting for me at her office door. "December, come in."

Cheryllynn walks in with me, and we both sit down in chairs right in front of Mrs. Vaca's desk.

"Miss Watts, why are you here?"

"For moral support." Cheryllynn leans forward and stares straight at her.

Principal Vaca ignores Cheryllynn and begins her lecture. "December, at Fairview Elementary we do not tolerate the kind of behavior you showed today. You can't jump off the monkey bars. You'll hurt yourself. I could let you off with a warning, but you also had the owl incident not too long ago. So I'm going to have to call your mom."

"She's not my mom."

Mrs. Vaca looks at her computer screen, which has my student information listed. "Eleanor . . ."

"She's my foster mom."

"Well, I'm calling her." Principal Vaca stares over at Cheryllynn. "Miss Watts, you can go back to class."

Cheryllynn pulls her hair back in a ponytail. "Mrs. Vaca, did you ever think that maybe at her other schools doing flips off monkey bars was an okay thing to do?"

"I'm pretty sure jumping off monkey bars is not permitted at other schools." Mrs. Vaca presses the phone to her ear.

If principals were birds, they'd be penguins. They'd live where it's cold, and they wouldn't be able to fly.

"Are Jenny and her friends going to get in trouble?" Cheryllynn asks. "Because they should. If they don't, I think it'd say a lot about your character, Mrs. Vaca."

Out of all the birds, Cheryllynn is most like a flamingo. She likes pink. She has long legs. And flamingos feed in mudflats or lagoons, so they are experts at stirring mud to find their food. I have a feeling, after watching the way the Vultures treat Cheryllynn and the way she stands up for herself, and for me, that she knows how to make her way through the mud.

"I can call your mom, too, if you'd like, Miss Watts?" Mrs. Vaca leans back in her chair. Her hair is spiked at the ends. It makes her look tough.

"Go ahead and call." Cheryllynn starts biting her pinky nail. "She'll tell you she can't come get me till school's out because she can't get out of work. I'd just have to sit in the office all day."

It's quiet, which is weird in a principal's office because principals always have something to say.

Mrs. Vaca dials Eleanor's number, and Cheryllynn gets up without waiting for her to tell us we can leave. "Come on. Let's wait outside."

We sit in the two chairs we sat in before.

"Nothing ever happens to Jenny," Cheryllynn whispers. "Her dad helped build the new cafeteria, and her mom's always down here volunteering."

Mrs. Vaca's office door opens. "December, Eleanor will be here in a few minutes. Miss Watts, you may go back to class. Now, please."

There's a red-and-black cardboard treasure box on the front counter. "Mrs. Franca," Cheryllynn says, "can I have a character slip?"

Mrs. Franca, the school secretary, reaches into a drawer and slides a blue paper toward Cheryllynn. "And a pencil, please." Cheryllynn writes my name on the slip and drops it through a slit at the top of the treasure box. "This is the Character Trait box. This month we're supposed to write down people who showed compassion. If they draw your name, you win a prize."

I step up to the counter, write Cheryllynn's name on a slip, too, and drop it in the box.

When Eleanor gets here she's probably going to be mad that I interrupted her day. It's not the first time a foster parent has had to come pick me up at school. They usually let someone know they're here and don't say anything to me as we leave. At their house, I'm grounded, or I have to do chores, or they take away privileges. The bad ones yell. Maybe Eleanor will make me sit in her shed and watch her stuff a bird.

But as she walks into the office, Eleanor doesn't look mad. She lets Mrs. Franca know she's here to pick me up and doesn't say a word until we get to the truck. "You had a hard day, huh?"

I tell her about the Vultures and how they treated me and Cheryllynn. I'm waiting for Eleanor to say the usual: "Well, life's unfair. You should try to stay away from them next time, and if they try to start trouble, go tell an adult instead of trying to take care of it yourself."

She rests both her hands on the top of the steering wheel. "You know what the most courageous bird is?"

"Of course I do. It's a bird you wouldn't expect."

Eleanor smiles. "Right, because we see them pretty much every day, so we don't notice them."

I smile, too. I can't help it. It's nice to be around someone who knows about birds like I do. "It's the crow."

They're fierce birds and have been known to chase bald eagles. Crows will drop stones or pine cones on predators, or even on people. They have a great memory, and they are as smart as parrots. They've been known to use sticks as tools, and have the ability to problem-solve.

At first I think Eleanor is going to put her arm around

me, but she rests it on the back of my seat and leans forward. "You were a crow today," she says, "and you should take that as the greatest of compliments."

On the way home, Eleanor sings, of course, mumbling or humming when she doesn't know the words to a song. It's a nice sound.

"Tomorrow's Halloween." Eleanor sings these words, too. "You haven't said anything about it, but would you like to go get a costume?"

"No, I don't want one. I don't like going trick-or-treating." I don't see the point of spending more time walking up to strangers' houses because I've done it pretty much all my life. "Is that okay?"

"That you don't like going trick-or-treating? Of course it is."

I wait for Eleanor to ask why I don't like trick-or-treating, and then try to give me reasons why I should go, like "But you'll miss out on all the fun" or "You're only a kid once."

"If you change your mind, let me know. I'd dress up with you."

"You'd dress up? What would we be?"

"Crows?" Eleanor smiles.

The image of us dressed as crows makes me smile, too.

"But I'm happy with staying home. Either way is fine."

"You'd dress up with me, right?"

"I would."

"Well, I'd go trick-or-treating just to see you dress up."

"Okay, then, let's go find some costumes."

Halloween night, before leaving to go trick-or-treating, Eleanor and I set up our jack-o'-lanterns on the front porch. We place tea lights inside, and from the end of the driveway the pumpkins glow orange.

Eleanor drives into town and parks the car at the edge of a subdivision. There are silhouettes of skeletons, princesses, zombies, and superheroes. But Eleanor is a witch, and I am a ghost. I didn't like any costumes left at the store, so Eleanor used an old bedsheet to make me one.

Kids pass, their feet shuffling across cement, or scampering across grass. Mine don't want to move.

I have no problem climbing to the highest branch of a tree, so walking up to a stranger's house and asking for candy should be easy. Eleven-year-olds don't need their mom, or dad, or foster parent to hold their hand to go trick-or-treating. A normal eleven-year-old should be able to go up to a house, say, "Trick or treat," and not worry whether a grown-up will have disappeared by the time she returns, leaving the eleven-year-old by herself.

My trick-or-treat bag is a pillowcase with red and brown leaves on it that Eleanor gave me. "Will you walk up to the door with me?" I ask.

"Of course," Eleanor whispers in her Bird Whisperer voice. I realize I'm starting to kind of like it.

I almost grab her hand, wondering if the feeling of holding it would be warm like a nest.

Our feet shuffle up the sidewalk, together.

17

Thanksgiving morning, Eleanor and I are in the field with Henrietta. She's calmer today, which is a good sign.

"I know you're nervous," Eleanor says to me. "Just remember, if Henrietta isn't cooperating, we keep trying."

I'm more scared than nervous. I'm scared that Henrietta won't ever fly. I'm scared that I won't ever fly, either.

I raise my arm, and she hops onto the perch. "After we're finished out here," I tell Henrietta, "we have a special Thanksgiving treat for you."

Henrietta's deep brown eyes stare at me like she understands what I'm telling her.

"Let's try about ten yards," Eleanor says.

I place pieces of raw meat on my glove and move my arm up and down, ringing the bell. Henrietta doesn't push off right away. She flutters her wings, still not sure.

"Come on, Henrietta, you can do this." I wave my arm up and down again. "Please, just fly," I whisper.

Henrietta spreads her wings, pushes off the perch, and swoops downward. At first, it looks like she's going to land on the ground, but she swoops upward and lands on my glove.

My heart soars. "Good job," I whisper.

Eleanor keeps having me move a little farther away, until Henrietta's last flight is about twenty yards from perch to perch. But it doesn't matter how far she flew this morning, it just matters that she flew.

As we're walking toward the refuge, Eleanor says, "She still has a ways to go, but today feels like we're back on track."

Henrietta screeches like she agrees.

At the back of the rehabilitation center is a big cage with wooden, branch-like perches and more space for Henrietta to move. I set Henrietta on one of the perches inside the cage. She puffs out her chest and spreads both wings.

"Let's go get Henrietta's surprise." Eleanor leads me to an area where there's a small refrigerator, a sink, and some cupboards. On top of the counter is a small cardboard box. Eleanor brings the box to the cage. There are mice inside. Even the way she handles the mice is gentle, and I wonder if she's gentle because she knows what's going to happen to them, or because they're animals, too. Like, is Eleanor being kind to me because she's read my file and knows about my past, or would she treat any kid, no matter what happened to her, the same?

"Happy Thanksgiving, Henrietta." Eleanor lets me set the mice on the floor of the cage. They scurry to any hiding place they can find. "Henrietta shouldn't miss an evolutionary beat. Her instinct to hunt is, well, instinctual. But we need to see if she's strong enough to catch food. She might not be hungry right now, so the next time we come to check on her, we'll have to search to find whether the mice are still here or not."

It's hard to imagine myself perched on a tree limb, or electrical wire, or fence, focused on the movement of prey, and being as still as Henrietta is now. The only time I remember being that still is the night my mom left. I remember lying on the floor. I remember watching my mom's feet walk back and forth from the living room to her bedroom. She threw clothes in a suitcase. They fell through the air like snowflakes. The air was cold. The door was open, and it was still open after her feet walked out into the night.

"You ready to go?" Eleanor sets her hand on my shoulder, and I step back. I don't want to be touched. My heart beats fast, faster than Henrietta's will when she sees the movement of mice and by instinct knows it's the right time to swoop down and clutch prey with her talons. *It's not my mom's touch. Eleanor's doesn't hurt at all.*

I lean into Eleanor's stomach. Her shirt smells like lavender and the air outside, her clothes and skin carrying the smell of leaves, trees, and rain. Her stomach is like a hummingbird's nest, and I can't burrow far enough into the warmth and softness.

Eleanor is like a hundred-year-old live oak tree. She stays until my heartbeat is back to normal, until the only thing I see is her brown sweatshirt and her blue-green veins rising from her skin, not the image of my mom's clothes falling through the air, or her feet walking out the door.

Eleanor gives me a gentle squeeze. She doesn't make a big deal out of my moment of weakness, and on the drive home she doesn't ask if I want to talk about what I was feeling. Instead, we listen to music. When we get home, she goes to the kitchen to start making soup for our Thanksgiving dinner, and she lets me wander out to the backyard. I like that she just lets me be, and trusts that I'll come to her if I need to. And I like that I trust her to be there when I do.

I check the feeders to see if they need to be filled with more seeds. There are three sparrows perched in a small, delicate tree, waiting for me to leave so they can eat.

I open the back gate. The scarecrow I made from leaves

and twigs is still standing. It doesn't matter if it really does scare away birds. It's not needed now. The Bird Whisperer is not a threat.

I pull the scarecrow out of the dirt and lean it against the fence. Behind me, I feel Teresa staring down at me from the highest branch of my flight tree. She doesn't need to be there anymore, either.

Climbing to the branch just below where Teresa's perched, I hold up *Bird Girl*. "I have it back!" I tell her. I open my story.

> December sat on the floor for a long time before she moved, watching the leaves swirl in a mini-tornado, blowing through the open door. She pulled herself across the floor to the leaves, picking them up, making a bouquet. They were mostly brown, but a few still had yellow and red color left in them. If she could've, December would've found a cup. She would've set the bouquet inside for her mom to see when she came back.

I close the book. Looking down makes my stomach nauseous. There are a lot of branches between the ground and me. There is a lot of space, too. Space to fall.

It's not something I was ever afraid of, until now.

Holding on to a branch, I shove the book into my back pocket and reach up to get Teresa. From here, I pull myself over the branch, my eyes even with hers. I reach around the trunk and pull the socks loose. Teresa drops forward, and before I can catch her, she falls, hitting branches on her way down. One of her talons flies through the air, and other parts, too—her beak, one of her glass eyes.

Instead of jumping, I climb down, and search for the broken parts. Broken parts are what can happen if something falls from way up high. I know that. I pick up the beak, and the glass eye, cradling them in my hand, and stare at the pieces.

Inside the house, Eleanor is getting the table ready, setting red plates and bowls at our places.

"I'm sorry. I shouldn't have taken her without asking."

I lay Teresa on the table and hold out my hand so Eleanor can see the broken pieces. "I thought she needed to be set free. She looked sad, all dusty sitting in your shed. I'll fix her, if you show me how, and I'll put her back where you had her."

When she frowns, Eleanor has the same line between her eyebrows as Karen, except Eleanor's isn't as deep and doesn't look like a claw. Hers is more a thinking line than an angry one, but I still wait for her voice to be filled with disappointment. Me breaking Teresa could be a reason to call Adrian, to send me away. But I'm ready, I'm always ready.

"Well, I'm not happy you took it without asking, but I'll show you how to fix it." Eleanor shakes Teresa's broken parts in her hand like she's about to roll dice. "It doesn't have to go back to the shed, either. You can keep it in your room, if you want?"

Eleanor leaves the bird in the middle of the table. "Why did you name her Teresa?"

"Well, one of my foster parents talked about saints a lot. There were two saints I really liked. I liked Saint Francis of Assisi because he's the patron saint of animals, but I loved St. Teresa because there are stories about her being able to levitate, and levitating is like flying."

Eleanor sets the glass eye and the other pieces on the counter. "Some things can't be put back together, but Teresa can. We'll do it after dinner."

I wonder what Eleanor believes she can't put back together.

She grabs both our bowls, filling hers all the way up and mine only three-quarters of the way. "In case you want to try it," she says. She places a basket of bread and some butter on the table, too.

"Should we say what we're thankful for?" Eleanor waves her hand over the bowl of soup and takes a deep breath.

"There's nothing better than the smell of leeks. Guess leeks are one thing I'm thankful for. But I'm most thankful for you coming into my life, December."

"You're not just saying that because it's Thanksgiving, are you?"

"No, I mean it. I hope you can stay with me for a long time."

"What's 'a long time'?"

"Guess forever would be a long time, right?"

"Yeah, it would be." I reach for the butter. "Eleanor, what did you mean by 'some things can't be put back together'?"

Eleanor sets her fork down and reaches into her back pocket. She takes a deep breath before holding up a picture.

The picture has white lines in a few places where it's been folded, and the color is faded, just like the one I carry of my mom. The girl in the photograph is younger than me, maybe the same age I was when I got the scar on my back. She's sitting on a bike, one hand gripping a handlebar, the other giving a thumbs-up sign.

She looks like Eleanor, her smile, the way she's squinting her eyes.

"That was my daughter." Eleanor places the picture in the middle of the table, leaning it against Teresa.

"It was a long time after she was gone that I could look at that picture." Eleanor's voice is almost a whisper. "It brought back too much sadness. But now, I look at it and I'm reminded of Sarah's smile, and how much she loved that bike. The past is tricky; you want to hold on to it, but you have to hold it at a distance, too, so you can see it clearly."

"What happened to her?"

"She got very sick." Eleanor holds a spoon and stares at her soup. Her eyes are watery.

She's lost someone, too. Someone she loved.

"Well," I say, changing the subject because I don't want Eleanor to cry, "I'm thankful we're not eating a turkey for Thanksgiving, because turkeys are incredible birds. Do you know turkeys have great geography skills? I read they can remember details of a piece of land as big as a thousand acres. That's a pretty big space for a turkey."

Eleanor closes her eyes as she takes her first sip of soup. It must taste good. I look down into my bowl. Even though staying here would make me happy, I know it won't be forever. I can't get used to warm soup. It'll just be something good that I'll have to leave behind.

"A lot of people think turkeys are flightless birds, and the ones that are raised to eat are, because they're too heavy. But wild turkeys can fly. Many domesticated birds, like the chicken and the duck, can't, but their ancestors were able to fly for long periods of time. Humans turned them into flightless birds. I think we should start a program where we take any flightless birds to the rehabilitation center and teach them to fly again."

Eleanor smiles. "Teaching them to levitate might be easier."

"True." I laugh, and the force of my breath makes ripples on the soup's surface. Laughing doesn't feel as strange anymore.

Eleanor pulls apart a piece of bread, dipping it in her soup. "And if you were a turkey, where in the world would you want to know in such detail?"

"I'd have to think about that." I copy Eleanor and dip a piece of bread in my soup. I stick out my tongue and touch the tip of it to the soggy part of the bread. I taste salt, just like when I eat sunflower seeds.

"You don't have to try it." Eleanor takes her bowl back to the stove and refills it. "I'd like you to like it enough to have some, but if you don't, you don't have to eat it."

I set the bread on a napkin. "Happy Thanksgiving, Eleanor."

"You, too, December."

After dinner, Eleanor comes back from her shed with a tube of superglue. "This is all we need to fix . . . What's her name?"

"Teresa." I lean over the counter, ready to watch Eleanor

glue the eye, beak, and talon back on the stuffed great horned owl.

Giving the superglue to me, Eleanor says, "Well, you broke it, so you have to fix it," but not in a mean way.

I squeeze a dab of glue onto the back of Teresa's eye. "I think the place would be Antarctica. That's the place I'd choose to know in detail, a place I'd know so well I wouldn't have to think about where I am."

"Antarctica?" Eleanor presses the eye in place. "Too cold for me."

"Cold is the point." I pick up Teresa's beak. "If I can learn to navigate my way around a place like Antarctica, anywhere else would be easy."

"Hmm . . . Maybe."

"What about you? Where would you pick?" I hold Teresa's beak against her face. "This house?"

Eleanor shakes her head and gives me the talon, the last broken piece. "It probably wouldn't be a country, a town or city. It wouldn't be a house, either. I prefer getting to know people. It's a lot like getting to know a place, except instead of streets, or buildings, or different landmarks, you get to know expressions, their tone of voice when they're feeling happy, whether they like to sing or like to just listen."

I lay Teresa on her side so the glue can dry on her talon.

"I already know a piece of geography about Eleanor Thomas."

"Okay." Eleanor raises her eyebrows, curious. "Let me hear it."

"Well, I know you snore, but it's soft, and as far as I know never gets loud enough to be annoying. You always seem to have dirt under your fingernails." I point to Eleanor's hands. "And because it's always there, I'm guessing you don't care. And, you sing. A lot. But, for the most part, you sing the same song. So, even though you probably like singing, it's the song you like more."

Tears fill Eleanor's eyes again, but not one drops. She wipes them away before they have a chance. "Now it's my turn. Let's see. When you eat sunflower seeds, you crack the shell open, then put the whole seed in your mouth, then spit out the shell. You stick your thumbs under the straps of your backpack when you walk to your classroom. The time you told me you never get cold, the tip of your nose and your cheeks were red."

Eleanor wraps her hands around mine. "And, you smile a lot more than you think you do."

"Do you believe Saint Teresa of Ávila really was able to levitate?"

"I have no idea. Here's what I do know—I don't think it matters all that much."

I pull my hands out from Eleanor's. "It matters a little, though."

"Why?"

"Because it means the impossible is possible."

Eleanor just nods, and caresses my cheek. "Guess it does," she says.

18

The first rain of December fills the birdbaths. The water is frozen this morning. I press my finger against the ice, draw zigzags, circles, write my name.

Leaves on trees, brown and heavy with water, shiver in the wind.

Teresa sits on the patio table, keeping watch. I sit down next to her. Eleanor's cooking bacon for breakfast. Even though I won't eat it, it smells good.

"It's cold today," I say to Teresa. "I know a lot about cold. My mom would leave the windows open in winter during the day, unless it was raining. I don't know if this is in my imagination, or if it really happened, but I remember fog drifting in through the windows. It was hard to see anything."

And there was never the smell of bacon. It always smelled like winter. The smell became part of my skin. It made sense, though. I was born in December. And with the front door and windows always open, the outside air absorbed into my skin and stayed.

"I'm used to the cold, though. Thanks to my mom. I think the real reason she left the door and windows open all the time was because she hoped I'd fly away on my own, away from her, so she wouldn't have to take care of me. She didn't like taking care of me. That's how I ended up here.

"But great horned owls like you start to nest in January and February. In the dead of winter, you guys raise families. So winter can't be so bad."

Eleanor sticks her head out the door. "Breakfast is ready."

I pick up Teresa. "But because of my mom, I can adapt to the cold easy. That's a good skill to have, just in case."

When Eleanor drops me off at school, I wave goodbye until I can't see the green of the truck anymore. Other kids are slamming car doors and yelling, "Goodbye, Mom!" or "Goodbye, Dad!"

It's so natural for them to say "Mom." I don't remember actually saying the word to anyone, even to my biological mom, so it would be weird to call someone that. I think it would take me a while to get used to the word.

This morning, Mrs. Beck talks to us about a poem written by a man named Robert Frost. The title of the poem is "Looking for a Sunset Bird in Winter." As far as I can figure out, it's about a bird that sits in a tree, singing like an angel, but now it's winter and the bird is gone.

"In your journals, I want you to write a response to the poem," Mrs. Beck says. "How does it make you feel? Or, what do you think is going on in the poem? You could also write about why you might think Robert Frost was inspired to write the poem. Later, I would like some of you to volunteer to read your responses. You have about twenty minutes. You may begin."

When time is up, Mrs. Beck asks us if there are any students who want to share their journal entries. No one raises their hands. Mrs. Beck scans the class, and her eyes land on me just as I push my hand into the air.

"December, thank you for volunteering." Mrs. Beck claps her hands together. "You can choose to stay seated, but I'd like you to stand up so everyone has a better chance of hearing you."

My knees are weak, but leaning against my desk helps. Once I start reading, my voice isn't shaky. "In 'Looking for a Sunset Bird in Winter,' Mr. Frost doesn't seem to care if his poem makes me feel sad or happy. The poem is about having hope. In the poem Mr. Frost knows the bird is gone during the winter, and he can't hear the bird singing. But it will be back in the spring, and I read that as Mr. Frost saying something about hope."

"Wow," Mrs. Beck says, "that was very good, December. Let's give her a round of applause."

The class claps. Mrs. Beck looks up at the clock. "Okay, we have a few more minutes before it's time to go. Does anyone else want to share?"

The classroom phone rings. "Room eight," Mrs. Beck says. "Okay. I'll give her the message.

"December, your mom's going to be late picking you up. She wants you to wait in the office."

I nod. "Mrs. Beck, Eleanor isn't . . . Never mind."

While Mrs. Beck reminds us about homework, I think about Robert Frost's poem.

Instead of waiting in the office, I stand outside, against the wall.

"Did Eleanor forget you?" Cheryllynn asks.

"No, she's just going to be late."

Cheryllynn pats the outside of her coat pockets. "Checking if I have any Froot Loops left."

Kids rush around us, jumping in cars and slamming doors. Cheryllynn stays with me until we're the only ones left standing in front of the school.

"I'll go into the office with you if you want to call Eleanor," Cheryllynn says.

I shake my head. "No, I'll give her some more time."

Mrs. Franca sticks her head out the office door. "Cheryl-lynn, sweetie, your mom's on the phone wondering if you're still at school."

"Can you tell her I'm walking to the store now? Thanks."

"Well, I better get going." As Cheryllynn walks across the parking lot, she keeps looking over her shoulder toward me. When she gets to the sidewalk, she turns around. "You sure you're going to be okay?"

I give her a thumbs-up. "Yes, I'll be fine."

But she must not hear me, because she runs back, opening the school office door. "I'll be a second."

While she's inside, I stare down the road, the direction Eleanor would be coming from. There's no truck heading this way. What if something happened to her? What if she's decided she doesn't want me to live with her anymore? What if it's Adrian, and not Eleanor, who comes to pick me up? I don't think I've done anything to give Eleanor a reason for leaving me here, but people leave without giving a reason all the time.

"Okay." Cheryllynn leans against the wall next to me. "I called my mom and asked if I could wait with you. She said yes, so you're stuck with me."

"I think I want to leave. I think I better go to Eleanor's house."

"I thought you said Eleanor was going to be here."

"I don't think she's coming to get me." I take off running, not caring if Cheryllynn is following me.

But when I get to the railroad tracks, I smell Froot Loops. "I said you were stuck with me," she says.

We turn down a canal bank. On the road, cars' headlights glow, and in the western sky, there's a little bit of orange light shining between blue clouds.

My and Cheryllynn's breaths make unidentifiable patterns against the air.

The closer we get to Eleanor's house, the more the wild blackberries and oak trees turn to shadows.

At the end of her driveway, I can't see Eleanor's truck. But the front yard is covered with Christmas decorations— a blow-up Santa, a blow-up snow globe with a reindeer inside, and a polar bear wearing a Santa hat and scarf. I've only seen these types of decorations in other people's yards. Eleanor could do all this, but she couldn't remember to pick me up?

I open the gate to the backyard.

"Where we going?" Cheryllynn asks.

I run out to the base of the tree and toss my backpack on the ground.

I balance on the third branch up, just like I did on the monkey bars, then crouch down. The bark scratches against my skin, but it doesn't hurt.

I take a deep breath, look down, and wave at Cheryllynn.

She doesn't wave back. "That's a little higher than the monkey bars."

"It's not that high."

"You're not going to jump, are you?"

"Why not jump?"

"What do you mean, 'Why not jump?' Because you could break something, that's why not."

"I won't break anything. Don't worry."

"I didn't say you 'would' break something, I said you 'could.' There's a difference. As much as I'd like to see your gymnastics talents again, I'd rather have you in one piece." I shuffle my feet closer to the edge of the branch and bounce a little.

"Maybe you could move down to the first set of branches," Cheryllynn says. "You don't have to prove anything to me."

The layer of skin over my shoulder blades tightens, bones and cartilage trying to escape.

"We have to stick together, December. You're my friend," she says.

I've learned to be a lone bird. There's a pattern in my life: people come and people go. No person has interrupted this pattern, except for Adrian, and he flies in, checks to see how I'm doing, and flies out again.

I slide back on the branch, lean against the trunk, and open *Bird Girl*. "My mom left me when I was little, and . . ." I'm ready to tell Cheryllynn my story. I read, *"December didn't close the door. She really thought her mom was coming back for her. All the smells from outside—dirt, rain, fog, gasoline, and hot dogs from down the block at Oasis Market—made her want to leave. Maybe December's mom left because she wanted December to find her wings again on her own. December did walk out the door, but it wasn't because she was going to try to fly. She left because she couldn't take smelling those hot dogs from Oasis Market anymore. She left home because she was hungry."*

I jump, but it's from the second tier, with not enough space between the ground and me to give my wings a chance to unfold.

"I'm sorry your mom left," Cheryllynn says.

"Well, at least the hot dogs tasted good," I lie.

Cheryllynn turns around and points to the backs of her thighs. "See right here? I have two scars that run across my legs. Long time ago, we used to live with my dad. He wasn't a nice person. Sometimes I'll come up with fairy-tale stories for how I got the scars, like 'Once upon a time, I was swimming in the river and my legs got tangled up with branches. The branches wouldn't let go, but a salmon swimming against the current freed me. The salmon saved my life. The branches left scars, but the rest of me was beautiful as always. The end.' Sometimes I'll change the fish to a trout. Sometimes I'll add some gruesome details to the story, like that I was caught in a blackberry bush at night, and an owl freed me. But I'll always remember how I really got the scars. The truth isn't a fairy tale."

It doesn't have to be a fairy tale. It could be a different kind of story. "Truth is overrated."

"Not always. You still have to know what the truth is, even if people—even if you—don't like it. I mean, I can imagine all I want about how I got my scars, but I don't ever want to forget how I got them, even if it hurts me to remember. My mom says remembering is still important because it can protect me from hurting more."

A door slams, and I hear Eleanor's boots scraping the sidewalk in the backyard, then the gate opens. "December?" She's running toward me. Her eyes are big, like an ostrich's.

"You're here." She's breathing hard. "You're here. You're okay. Didn't you get my message?"

"I waited at school for a long time, then I thought you weren't going to show up."

Eleanor kisses my forehead. She bends down so that we're eye to eye and rests her hands lightly on my shoulders. "I'm sorry," she says. "I lost track of time. Not a good excuse. I may have been late, but I didn't forget you. I will never forget you."

I nod. I want to believe her.

Since her mom's working, we drive Cheryllynn to the store. On the way back to the house, it's quiet except for Eleanor, who's humming "Eleanor Rigby," and the sound is sad, blue sad. "I didn't mean to scare you, December," she says.

She stops at a stop sign and pauses a little longer than she usually does. "I want us . . . I want you to be happy."

"You want *us* to be happy. *Us* is the word you used."

"Yes, I do want *us* to be happy."

As we're sitting in Eleanor's pickup truck, with the world surrounded by tule fog, making it hard to see in front of us, making the world feel heavier, my heart and the rest of me are light.

Us is a word like *Mom*. I know what it means. I know how to use it in a sentence. But it's a strange word. It's like when I'm standing on the ground, watching a bird soar in the sky. I know flight is out there, but there's a distance. Just like with *us*. There's a gap between the word and me.

19

I was born in the early morning, so by the time I wake up on my birthday, December 21, I'm already twelve. The house smells warm and sweet, and when I sit down at the kitchen table Eleanor sets a plate of cookies shaped like snowflakes in front of me. They're still warm. I take a bite of one and wash it down with hot chocolate.

"Happy birthday! How does it feel to be twelve years old?" Eleanor sits down with me and eats a snowflake in two bites.

"It feels different than when I turned eleven." And not because I live somewhere else.

Last year, on my birthday, I sat in a tree all day. Even when Wes and Linda called my name over and over again, I didn't move. I'd brought a bag of sunflower seeds, a Snickers bar I'd taken from Wes's candy stash, and a can of Pepsi up with me.

Before trying to fly, I stuffed the empty can, candy wrapper, and bag of seeds in my pocket, opened *Bird Girl*, and read the part about when I was a baby.

Whenever her mom held December, she'd breathe fast, like she wanted to hurry up and get the holding over with. It was like her mom was afraid, like she was riding on a roller coaster instead of holding a baby. When she put December down, her breath went back to normal. Then she'd look at December like moms are supposed to.

But December's mom always believed December would be capable of doing amazing and wondrous things.

Later in the day, instead of climbing my flight tree, I sit on the ground, against the trunk, and eat another snowflake. I open *Bird Girl* to the last page, where I've drawn an illustration of Amelia Earhart's first airplane, the *Canary*. Just in case my wings were a once-in-a-lifetime thing and when they went dormant, they were meant to stay that way, I had drawn some alternate plans for flight and made some notes about them. I never thought I'd need them, though.

WINGS

Possibility #1—Made from aluminum cans. Would need to find a motor to attach for propulsion. Drawback: Collecting aluminum cans wouldn't be the problem, but storing them and taking them from foster home to foster home would be.

Possibility #2—Made from birds' feathers (all types) collected from the ground. Drawback: It would take forever to collect the feathers I need to build a set of wings with a long enough wingspan* or wide enough wing area.

Possibility #3—Twigs/branches. Drawback: Collecting and storing again and, just like with set one and set two, a place to assemble and keep the wings. Probably wouldn't take as long to collect as feathers, but still would be a long process.

*Note: Wingspan would have to be
11 feet x 2 = 22 feet from wing tip to wing tip.

I turn to a blank page and draw a series of pictures. The first panel shows a five-year-old me, asleep under a tree.

The next panel shows footsteps, walking through leaves, and then a talking bubble with musical notes. The third panel is a woman, standing over me, saying (even though I'm just my normal-self, not my bird-self), "What a magnificent creature!" In the last panel, the woman picks me up in her arms, whispering, "My name is Eleanor."

I hear the gate close, and there's Eleanor in real life. I hurry before she gets out to the trees and shove *Bird Girl* into my backpack.

Eleanor's carrying a picnic basket and a blue blanket. "I was going to surprise you, but you're already out here."

She spreads the blanket on the ground and from the basket takes out blue plates and a ziplock bag of something else that's blue. "I made these last night," Eleanor says.

Inside the bag are origami birds. They're amazing. We hang them from the branches. When we're finished, my flight tree looks even more beautiful.

Eleanor sets a pink box in the middle of the blanket and opens the lid. There are cupcakes with blue frosting. She places one on each plate and then pulls a thermos filled with hot chocolate from her bag.

"Surprise!" a voice yells from behind me. It's Cheryl-lynn. "Happy birthday!"

She's wearing a sky blue dress with tights the same color, black boots, and a purple furry coat. "How'd you get here?"

I don't ask it to be mean. It's amazing she's here. Birthday parties in the past have usually been Adrian taking me out to dinner.

"My mom dropped me off." Cheryllynn holds out a package and sits next to me. Up above, fog is parting to show a winter blue sky. "You have to open my present now."

The present is wrapped in a brown paper bag decorated with different-colored birds. I unravel green tissue paper. Inside are the butterfly wings I tried on at Sav-Mor Market.

"They looked good on you at the store," Cheryllynn says. "So I thought you should have them."

I thread my arms through the wings. Eleanor lights a candle, and she and Cheryllynn sing "Happy Birthday" to me. It's the most beautiful song I've ever heard, more beautiful than a nightingale's.

Day is fading from the sky. Eleanor turns on a lantern and opens one of the little boxes decorated with snowflakes that are by each of our plates. "These," she says, "are winter solstice fortunes. It's my own tradition. I'll read mine first. 'In the darkness, there is always light.' I always get that one. It's a good reminder, though. Who wants to go next?"

Cheryllynn raises her hand. "I'll go." She reads the fortune. "'The one who makes it through the storm is the one who keeps walking.'"

I've gone through a storm before, except I didn't walk, I crawled, across the living room floor, down the steps of our trailer, across the cold ground, into the walnut orchard.

"You want to read next?" Eleanor sips hot chocolate from a teacup.

"Okay." I remember crawling to one of the trees in the orchard and curling up next to the trunk. I remember hearing cars driving by on the road, not far away. I kept breathing, and when I breathed out, I made a sound, a wounded sound. Before closing my eyes, I saw red drops on the ground, between the trailer park and me. I made myself think the drops were rain.

"Okay," I say again, and take a deep breath. Tears want to fall, too, but I don't let them. I open the box and pull out a slip of paper that says, " 'Snowflakes are beautiful and intricate. Be sure to look at them closely.' "

"That's a good reminder," Cheryllynn says.

"It is," I agree, and shove the winter solstice paper into my pocket, a birthday memento.

Eleanor takes my hand and squeezes it gently. I still brace myself a little, but instead of wanting to pull away, my hand rests in the warmth of hers. If I were to look at it under a microscope, I'd find amazing designs on Eleanor's skin. Patterns that had never been seen in nature before. There would be hearts, and scars that are shaped like birds and other animals. The designs and shapes would tell a story, like hieroglyphics on a cave wall.

If Eleanor looked at me under a microscope, she'd see faded photographs. There would be three. The first one would be the kindergarten photo of my mom; the next one would be a picture of me as a baby, my mom holding me in one arm, her eyes looking off to the side, away from me. The last picture would be of me on the day my mom left. I'd be lying inside the doorway, my arm out, waving goodbye.

But if Eleanor looked at my scar, there would be no photographs, or hieroglyphics. Or maybe there would be, but the images would be distorted and blurry. Maybe the only thing she'd be able to make out is a feather, just one, proof of nothing.

Eleanor gives my hand one more squeeze before letting go. "You are twelve years old," she says.

"I am." I always believed that by now, I would've had the ability to fly to the rain forest, or to Antarctica. But I also believed that there wasn't ever going to be anyone like Eleanor out in the world.

After Cheryllynn leaves, I help Eleanor take down the origami birds.

"Do you want to keep these?" she asks.

"Sure," I say. "I'll hang them in my room."

We gather the dishes, the blanket, and the birds, and

the whole time I wear the butterfly wings Cheryllynn gave me. I'm still wearing them when there's a knock at the door.

As soon as Adrian walks in he says, "Happy birthday! Sorry I'm late."

Even though the sky is gray now, and there's only a little bit of daylight left, we go out to the backyard.

"Eleanor gave me a party today. I like it here with her."

"I'm really glad, December."

And if you ever try to put me somewhere else, I'll just keep running back to wherever Eleanor lives.

"I can't believe you're twelve years old." Adrian gives me a present.

I unwrap the paper, which is decorated with feathers. It's a book, *Ornithology.*

"I don't know if there's anything you haven't taught yourself about birds, but I also know there's always something we miss along the way, questions we still need to have answered."

"Thanks." I open the book. It's different from *The Complete Guide to Birds: Volume One.* It has less photographs and more charts and diagrams.

"I have one more for you," Adrian says.

Inside a small blue box is a necklace with a silver bird for a charm.

While he hooks the clasp around my neck, I look out at some bluebirds. They're perched on the edge of the birdbath, staring at the water that was frozen this morning. "I really like it here with Eleanor," I say again. I want to make sure Adrian knows how I feel. "This is the first time I've wanted to stay with anybody. Maybe someday she might even decide to adopt me."

"That's good, December. I'm so glad." Adrian stares at the birds, his voice no longer green. Now, it's yellow. Not the happy sunshine yellow, but like the yellow at a stoplight.

It's habit, though. I think over time he's had to be cautious when it comes to finding a home for me. Adrian has natural balancing skills, too. He has to keep me hopeful, but be real about things at the same time.

"I'm so happy that you like being here with Eleanor." That's all he says, which is okay for right now.

Both of us watch the bluebirds. They dip their beaks in the water.

Water. It can freeze, melt, evaporate, but no matter its state, it always remains what it is. And, no matter my state, or no matter what the future is, I will always remain December Lee Morgan, extraordinary bird.

Later that night, after I brush my teeth and go into the living room to tell Eleanor good night, the telephone rings.

"Hello," Eleanor says. Whoever called is doing most of the talking. "I understand." Eleanor lowers her voice like she doesn't want me to hear what she's saying, but I can anyway. "Thirty days. Yes. Goodbye."

Her footsteps press harder against the floor, her pace slower. Sitting down, she stares at a flower-printed tablecloth.

"Did that call have something to do with the rehabilitation center?" I ask. I lean close to the table to try and look into Eleanor's eyes.

"No." Her voice is not Bird Whisperer–like. It's shaky again. "I don't know if Adrian told you, but I don't own this house. I rent it. The owners have decided to sell it, so I have to find another place to live."

I'm about to say, *Well, we can start looking for a place tomorrow*, but then realize Eleanor said, "*I* have to find another place to live." I start to feel like I did the day in the corn maze when I lost my sense of direction.

"I really loved living here," she says. "This place was perfect for me, but I guess it's time to move on."

Eleanor fills a kettle with water and sets it on the stove. I wait for her to say something about *us* finding a place to live, or to say, *We will look together, since you'll be living there, too.* But she doesn't. The water boils, she pours it into a cup, and she stands, dipping a tea bag up and down. She never says anything about *we.*

I know the story Eleanor is beginning to tell. It's the same beginning I've heard a hundred times, and it ends with people leaving me behind. My mom left without taking me with her—and it wasn't because she wanted me to find my wings again on my own. She left, and she's never tried to come back.

So I figured out a way to never get left behind again.

If I'm the first to leave, there's no chance of ever being left in a house, all alone, with a night sky shading the front door, and me, waiting.

I go to my room and take out *Bird Girl.* I've written my story. It's a reminder I was born with a half-human, half-avian heart, and that I, not Eleanor, not Adrian, not any of my other foster parents, get to choose what happens next.

I turn to the page titled "Flight."

All through the day, December waited for her
mom, until the windows turned blue, then black,
and the only sound was her heartbeat, beating
extra deep and fast. The door was still open, a cold
wind blowing through the house. December and

her heartbeat leaned over the edge of the steps
leading down to the trailer park road, and she
didn't wait. There was no one to tell her not to fly.

I'm not going to pack my clothes, and I'm going to leave my orphan dolls behind. I won't need them. What I'll need is to travel lighter than I've ever traveled.

There's a knock on my door. "December? You ran into your room so fast. Do you want to talk about it?"

There's nothing left to say. Eleanor doesn't have a home anymore; wherever she goes, she won't be taking me with her.

Eleanor knocks again. "December." She's using her Bird Whisperer voice. "Please."

"I just want to be by myself."

"I'll find a place . . ."

"You lied to me," I whisper. She shouldn't have said, *I will never forget you.* She shouldn't have talked about *forever.* I wrap my pillow around the back of my head, covering my ears. I don't want to hear . . . I *can't* hear Eleanor's, the Bird Whisperer's, words anymore. This is not part of my story.

She's still trying to talk to me, but the sound is muffled. I let myself believe I could have a home, but there are only two truths I know for sure now: One, maybe there's no such thing as home for me. And two, it doesn't matter. Because I'm an extraordinary bird.

She once said that the past was tricky. It isn't. She said to not hold it too close, but I do, because it reminds me of who I am. It helps me remember the words my mom wrote in my guidebook, "*In flight is where you'll find me*," and why I have to find my wings. I know when I fly I'm not going to find my mom. I don't want to. Maybe at some point I did, but all that's happened has changed that. I think the quote was her way of saying that no matter where I go, she'll always be with me.

I keep the pillow pressed against my ears and whisper, "*I will fly*," over and over again, waiting until Eleanor's words have stopped. I don't have time for her anymore.

I peek out into the hallway. Eleanor's bedroom door is open but her light is off. I listen for any sound coming from the kitchen. It's quiet.

I tiptoe down the hallway to use the bathroom. Washing my hands, I look at my reflection in the mirror. The mirror hangs high on the wall, so I only see half my face, from my nose to the top of my head.

I lift strands of my hair. I haven't let anyone cut it in a couple of years. I did let Adrian take me to a hair salon once, but on one condition—I got to keep all the hair the lady cut. I walked out of the salon with a plastic bag full of my hair, but then left it at a foster parent's house.

But my hair is heavy now, and heavy isn't good for flight.

I find a pair of scissors in a kitchen drawer, go back to the bathroom, and cut fast. I don't have to have even ends. I'm not cutting my hair for beauty. I'm cutting it for egress.

Hair drops around my feet. I gather all of it, even the smallest of strands, and flush it down the toilet.

I'm not sure how to end *Bird Girl*. I could have December live a happily-ever-after bird's life, flying all over the world, spending time in the rain forest with toucans, or visiting Antarctica and huddling with emperor penguins.

Or I could have December be braver than she ever thought she could be, and not worry about whether wings will unfold from her scar, and instead go into Eleanor's room and offer to help find a place to live. And maybe Eleanor would invite her to stay.

Or December could sneak out of the house, whisper, "Goodbye," blowing a kiss to Eleanor, and then fly across the yard.

And the very end will read like this: *As soon as December*

felt the cold against her skin, it was like she was home again. A half-moon hovered in the sky, lighting her flight tree. The moonlight was a sign it was time for December to find her wings, time for her to find her real home.

20

I read in my book that Canada geese return to the place where they were born to lay their eggs. If I had a choice where to be born, I might've chosen to be born in Eleanor's house, and for the rest of my life Eleanor would've protected me from storms and predators.

I look at the photograph of my mom, her kindergarten one, but there isn't anything familiar, except for the ways— eyes, hair, color of my skin—I look like her.

I pull myself over the first tier of branches.

The trick is to keep looking up, even though Adrian's told me a million times, "You need to look down sometimes, December, even if it's just to make sure your shoelaces are still tied."

I stop at the second tier. Above me a little fog moves in, coloring pieces of the sky white. I take a deep breath. Beyond moonlight, there is a wall of dark space I'll be flying into. I wonder how long I'll have to fly before I see sunlight.

I hold tight to the branches and keep climbing.

On July 2, 1937, while trying to fly around the world, Amelia Earhart and her navigator, Frederick Noonan, lost their way somewhere in the middle of the Pacific Ocean and disappeared. Some people think they survived on an island somewhere, or that they were rescued and lived the rest of their lives under different names. I think they became birds.

I look up to the branches above me, to determine which one will be best. The fog makes them hard to see. I climb anyway. I know the tree well enough.

When I'm a bird, I'll fly to Cheryllynn's doorstep and she won't think anything of it. She won't be afraid to walk down the street holding the tip of my wing. If I offer, she'll hop onto my back and we'll fly past layers of clouds to find blue sky, and she'll never ask how I became a creature that could really fly.

When I get to the end of the right branch, my heart will push my wings through skin, and I will fly. Once I'm in the air, I'll miss the cold, gray world below, but my eyes will be on the winter sun—I'll fly over the horizon for a peek—and my feathers will soak up its warmth.

As I climb higher, my heart beats faster. It's the heart that controls the body's transformation.

Branches are smaller, less thick, up high. I'm more careful where I place my feet and hands. Moisture from the fog has made the tree wet and slippery.

There are three more tiers of branches till the top. My breath is fast, the rest of my body warm. This is high enough.

I lean against the trunk, still holding tight, still not looking down. There's only one sound. My heartbeat. It echoes loud enough Eleanor can probably hear it. I breathe cold air. It hurts my throat. My whole body twitches with my heartbeat.

I will fly.

Between beats, a twig snaps on the ground, the sound coming from the river in the distance. "Eleanor?" I wait for her voice to say, *December! December! December! You belong on the ground with me! Come down!*

"December?" Eleanor's robe glows in the light of the moon.

"I'm up here." My hands are still holding tight to branches. I let go a little and feel my body lean forward. The skin over my scar is warm and getting warmer, the muscles, ligaments, bones beginning to twist into place.

"Come down," she says between short breaths.

"I can't."

"Why not? You climbed up there. You can climb down."

Eleanor stands with her hands on her hips, like a strong tree, or like Wonder Woman, the robe her cape. "I don't want you to jump."

"But I have wings." The words sound weird out loud, like they don't belong to me anymore.

"I understand why you like birds so much. I really do." Eleanor looks up. Moonlight, shining behind me, filters through fog. "I mean, if I had a choice, I don't think it's the animal I'd pick. Flying would be amazing, but I think I'd miss the ground too much. I don't know what animal I'd be. Maybe I'd just stick to being human."

"Being human is too complicated. All you have to do when you're a bird, or reptile, or any other animal, is survive." I slide closer to the trunk of the tree. "You don't have to worry about people not being there for you, or leaving and never coming back." I try to make Eleanor understand. "If you could be an animal, what would you be? And being human isn't a choice."

"Okay. I've always wanted to be a whale, swimming in the ocean all day. But then"—Eleanor places her hand on the trunk of the tree and looks up—"I'd miss out on nursing injured animals back to health, and I wouldn't be able to eat cookies or soup."

A coyote howls in the distance. The sound is sad, but filled with the will to keep going, too.

"I'd take being able to fly over cookies any day. What's more amazing than being able to fly anywhere you wanted?"

"I think I'd still choose cookies."

"I don't really want to talk about cookies." I slide out again, farther on the branch. I can still see Eleanor from here. "I'm tired of having to hide my scar. The scar is really where my wings poked through my skin, and now I have to make them unfold again."

"I want you to come down," Eleanor repeats.

The coyote howls. Still sad. Still surviving.

"If you do have wings, December, there's a different way to make them unfold besides jumping out of trees. Please come down."

"I can't. It's not how my story is supposed to go."

"You can change your story. Like maybe you were born a bird but are evolving into a human?"

"I don't think so." But . . . I've never looked at my evolution that way before.

I've made up my mind. I'm going to fly. It's time. I close my eyes and chant, "*Feathers, feathers, feathers.*"

"I'm coming up there," Eleanor says. She and her glow-in-the-dark robe pull themselves over the first branch.

"But you're afraid of heights."

"I'm coming up there anyway." Standing, she reaches for the next tier of the tree, her foot slipping.

I hear her hit the ground. Hear her say, "That hurt."

It does hurt. I know. Even though I've talked myself into thinking falling doesn't hurt, it does. It does hurt. "Eleanor? You okay?"

I can't see her. "Eleanor! Can you hear me? Eleanor?"

"I'm fine," she says, "but you really need to come down, December. I'll stay here all night if I have to."

She won't have to stay out here all night. I'm going to fly.

The only creatures that will see my amazing feat are the owls and Eleanor. I'll be their midnight feature performer, a strange sight, a once-in-a-lifetime show, like Amelia Earhart's takeoffs and landings, or the resurrection of a long-lost mother.

I can't think too much about the quiet, or about Eleanor. The life I'm leaving behind is the same as always anyway, a life living between houses. It turns out Eleanor's was just another one of those houses, too.

I slide out on the limb farther. I'm as far as I need to go. My heart is ready. My breath is ready. The rest of me shakes a little. Adrian told me if I was ever in trouble, and there wasn't anyone around to help, I should scream, throw my arms in the air, and run, if I had to. I can't run now, though. But I don't need to. This is where I belong.

I close my eyes. All I need are my wings, plus maybe a little lift from the wind.

On three.

One. I won't fall. Not this time.

Two. I wish Eleanor would sing right now.

Three. I will fly.

I hover at first. I do, and I almost call out to the owls, "Do you see me now? What do you think?"

I fly until "six one thousand." But owls know the truth, like I do deep down: that everything falls, eventually.

I drop like rain, and see a blur of green below me. It's Eleanor's robe. She has her arms spread out, waiting, standing between me and the ground.

"I'll catch you!" is the last thing I hear before I fall on Eleanor. Her robe is soft against my head.

I am not a bird. My bones aren't aerodynamic. I think Amelia Earhart was wrong: it doesn't matter from what direction you're looking at a tree, as long as you stop and look.

"December, I'm here," Eleanor whispers. She presses her ear to my chest. My heart is still beating.

"I'm here." Two words. Simple. Like feathers, they give me warmth.

"December." The world spins a little, but I see her face. "You're going to be okay," she says. She caresses my cheek, and I don't flinch, my muscles don't tighten, my first instinct is not to fly away. "Try not to move."

Try not to move? But I don't know how not to move. Home to home. Parents to parents. Branch to branch.

Eleanor dials nine-one-one on her cell phone.

After hanging up, she leans close to me, and like the Bird Whisperer she is, whispers, "The social weaver birds' nests have chambers, and depending on where they're located and how deep they are in the mass of the nest, the chambers can protect the birds from the cold and heat."

I hear a siren in the distance. This time there's no place to jump; instead, with the arm I can move, I reach for Eleanor's hand and hold it like it's the last feather on the last bird that ever lived.

21

I wake up looking at a white ceiling and hearing voices that seem far away. Between the voices, there's a beeping sound, my own heart beating, in a normal, human rhythm.

If I open my mouth, I won't sing like a bird. I was never supposed to. I am not a bird. I am not even bird-like. My mom knew this. I was born a normal, everyday baby.

"December," Eleanor whispers. She's blurry, too, but I can tell she's smiling at me.

A doctor lifts one of my eyelids and shines a light. "Can you hear me, December?" the doctor says. I nod. *Yes, with my human ears I can hear everything you're saying.*

"How many fingers am I holding up, December?" the doctor asks. "How old are you, December? When is your birthday? What town do you live in?"

I don't know how much time has passed since my last attempt at flight, but I'm sure I turned twelve. I know I fell. I dropped from the sky like a raindrop.

"She's lucky she just has a sprained ankle and a broken wrist," the doctor says to Eleanor. "Even though her MRI scan doesn't show signs of a concussion, I want to observe her for a day or so, just in case. She's lucky she had you to break her fall."

My bones aren't light and flexible. They're the same as those of every one of these people standing in the room, just smaller.

Adrian walks through the door and stands by my bed. "December" is all he says.

The doctor listens to my heart. I'm sure he'll conclude my heartrate is in the normal range for a human. "Sounds good. I'll come by tomorrow to check up on you. Make sure you get some rest."

I hadn't noticed before, but there's a cast on my left arm, from my elbow to my wrist.

As I try to get up, it's hard not to think about falling.

"Take it easy," Eleanor says, sliding her arm across my shoulders.

There's a bruise on her cheek. The color of sky and soil combined. "Is that my fault?"

"I'm fine."

Eleanor doesn't look "fine." Her face is scratched up, and there's another bruise on the side of her forehead.

"I'm sorry," I say. "I didn't mean to hurt you."

Eleanor helps me lie back down. "I know you didn't. Just rest right now."

"I am tired."

Thoughts drift in and out as Christmas carols play through the speakers above me. I remember one Christmas. I think I was living with Louise and Frank, who didn't want to waste money on a Christmas tree. A week after the holidays, neighbors pulled their trees out to the street; I stole one, dragged it into the nearest orchard, and decorated it with pine cones and whatever else I could find and sat under it writing my story.

The book. My biography. "Where's my book?" I ask.

Eleanor holds up *The Complete Guide to Birds: Volume One.* "It's here."

"No, the one that was in my back pocket."

Eleanor slides open a drawer to a table that's next to my bed. "This one?"

I want to ask her to open it to the first page and read it to me.

I want to hear the fictional story of my life so far.

Adrian stares at my hands. They scraped branches on my way down. The scratches will be kindred spirits to the scar on my back. I should ask the doctor for a microscope, to see if there's writing in the scarred skin, like the words my mom wrote in my guidebook. But instead of saying, "In flight is where you'll find me," they should say, "Find a place you can call home."

The only things in *Bird Girl* I didn't create were the illustrations pasted at the beginning. Those were with "December's things," supposedly sketched by the boy who carried me to Oasis Market after finding me in the orchard. I must've looked like a baby bird that had fallen from its nest. I had to believe I was something different, miraculous, because I know, well, I remember enough to know the real story of my scars.

This time I close my eyes, but my dreams aren't filled with falling, or with flying, or with wings, or feathers. I'm sitting on the ground, against a tree, my flight tree. I'm writing in my book. I'm not writing a story. I'm writing a list of words, filling the pages with *miraculous, amazing, friend, normal, just, girl, home.* They're pieces to a new story.

I sleep, and when I open my eyes this time, Adrian and Eleanor aren't here, or I can't see them in the sea of spinning blue origami birds, the ones from my birthday party, now hanging from the ceiling of my hospital room. "Eleanor?" I say.

My voice sounds like it's been covered with rocks and dirt. "Eleanor," I say again, just to make sure it's my voice.

Eleanor walks into my room holding one of the origami

birds. "December." She says my name like she's known me all my life. She stands up on a chair and hangs the bird. "Got to get as many up as I can before they tell us to take them down."

The swaying of the birds reminds me of Henrietta. "How is she? How is Henrietta? We're going to fall behind. We'll have to start over, won't we?"

"She's fine." Eleanor steps down. "She's waiting for you to come back and finish training her."

I turn my head and look past a Christmas wreath with blue lights, to the sky, always the sky. It's going to take me a while to break this habit.

"When you talked about finding a house, you said, '*I* have to find another place to live.' Did you really mean *we*? Because . . ." I'm talking like I haven't talked my whole life, talking as if my life depends on it, which as far as I'm concerned it does.

". . . I'll run . . ."

I don't say *fly*.

". . . to wherever you are, Eleanor."

The birds above Eleanor's head swirl in the air coming through the ceiling vents. "You don't have to turn into a harpy eagle to keep me, December. You can stay with me as long as the home we find is a good place for you to live. When I got the phone call saying I had to move, you were always going to come with me."

I try to lift my left arm out from under the blankets, to give Eleanor a hug, but it's too sore. "Did you try to tell me that the other night?" I ask.

"I did," Eleanor says. "When you were in your room."

"I didn't want to hear you. It's my fault for . . ."

"It's not your fault, December. I'm sorry for not making myself clear.

"Look . . ." Eleanor holds up a present. "It's a belated birthday gift."

She unwraps the present. "Your teacher called me. She said you read a journal entry to the class. It was in response to a poem. She said your comments about the poem were very insightful. I'm proud of you, December."

The book is a collection of Robert Frost poems, mostly about nature.

"'Looking for a Sunset Bird in Winter' is in here." Eleanor turns to the title page and shows me an inscription. *"You're my 'piercing little star.' Always remember that. Love, Eleanor."*

I stare up at the ceiling. "The origami birds are pretty. Thanks for bringing them. Can you hand me my journal?"

As Eleanor opens *Bird Girl*, careful to turn to a blank page, there's a knock on the door. A man dressed as Santa Claus pops his head inside the room.

"It's almost Christmas," Eleanor whispers.

Santa Claus gives me a candy cane and asks what I want for Christmas. I can't tell him what I want, but I can tell him what I don't want. "Scratch the lifetime supply of sunflower seeds, bugs, and worms off my list."

Eleanor laughs.

When Santa leaves, she folds her hands over the book, holding a pen ready to write. All I say are the words, "My scar . . ." and the space between my shoulder blades starts hurting. But it's just a normal scar, hiding nothing but bones, blood, and the memory of my mom that night.

My voice cracks, and I hold the word *Mom* in my throat as long as I can before I have to let it out. "Once upon a time . . ."

No, not *once upon a time*. I take a deep breath. "This is what happened to me."

"I was eight years old."

Eleanor reaches for my hand.

"I don't think my mom knew what to do with me. She hurt me. Really bad. And then she left. And, never came back."

I cry, but the tears don't stop my words. "The door was already open. I saw her shoes leave. Flip-flops she wore even in winter. I was barefoot, but it didn't matter because I crawled to the door and almost slid down the steps. The cold ground took away the hurt in my back. I stared at bare branches and wished I was perched on one of them and able to fly away. A boy found me. And now, I'm here."

"Yes, you are," Eleanor says, moving the book so her own tears don't fall on the pages.

Blue from the origami birds covers the space, creating a blurred sky. I'll never get tired of birds. They're amazing creatures, from herons and their stillness to owls and their secrets of flying to hummingbirds and their acrobatics.

Eleanor closes the book. I like how she doesn't say she's sorry, or how terrible that must've been to live through, or anything about life being hard for me. "You're right, you're here now," she says, and caresses my cheek. I don't flinch. My muscles don't twitch. Maybe they've finally lost the memory to do so.

Most of the origami birds are still now. "Can you get some pink paper?" I ask.

"How 'bout some white paper and a pink crayon?"

"That'll work. And, maybe, can you let Cheryllynn know where I am? I'd like to see her. And Adrian. Can you tell him I want to talk to him?"

Eleanor smiles like that jack-o'-lantern she and I carved together. "I'll be right back."

Eleanor opens the door. Cheryllynn, wearing her furry coat and carrying cups, one in each hand, can't get into the room fast enough.

"I'm glad you're here." I guess I can officially call Cheryllynn my best friend.

"Slushies." Cheryllynn holds the two cups in the air, and then sets them on a stand next to my bed. "So, you look to me like you're going to be okay."

I point to my cast. "A broken wrist. Probably could've been worse if Eleanor hadn't been there. She tried to catch me."

"She seems like the kind of person who would do that."

"Yes, she does."

Cheryllynn looks up to the birds hanging from the ceiling. "Are those the same ones from your party?"

I nod. "Did you know scientists believe that birds evolved from theropod dinosaurs? So now, when you see a bird, you can tell people that you saw a living dinosaur."

Cherllynn responds, "I'm definitely going to start saying that."

Eleanor walks in the room with paper and crayons, and I stare at Cheryllynn. Both their clothes, hair, their hearts, everything about them is designed to reflect who they are, no matter what.

They color papers pink, then Eleanor shows Cheryllynn how to fold them, and Eleanor stands on a chair and pins the pink birds to spaces in the ceiling between the blue ones.

If Dr. S asked right now what home meant to me, I hope the image of a nest wouldn't be the first thing to pop in my head. I hope I'd hear the sound of Eleanor singing first, then maybe a picture of her reading a poem about not one "piercing star," but two.

Maybe this is how I can end *Bird Girl*: *When December fell on the ground, she hit hard. She lay there, staring up at the sky. There were clouds, and she tried to look for ones shaped like birds, an albatross, a hawk, an everyday backyard swallow. But there was only one cloud shaped like anything she recognized. The cloud was shaped like a house, not a nest.*

There's a knock on the door. Adrian comes in and stares up at the birds. "Wow. Beautiful."

Eleanor and Cheryllynn leave, and Adrian sits on the side of my bed. "You look like you're doing okay."

I take a sip of my slushy. "Eleanor says that even though she has to move, I can move with her. Is that right?"

"Yes, that's right."

"Good, because I want you to know that I want to stay with Eleanor for a long time, okay?"

Adrian nods.

Bird Girl is lying next to me. "Can you turn to page forty-eight and start reading from the top?"

Adrian flips the pages.

"Being a bird is a lonely business. It's important that December makes sure not to get close to anyone. This might seem sad, but not for a bird. Getting close to people can make December's spirit heavy, making flight harder."

Adrian clears his throat. His eyes fill with tears.

He starts reading again.*"When December evolves into a bird, her memories will fade away. She won't remember the sound of her mother's voice, or remember toys she had, or smells, or certain clothes she wore. Her human senses will disappear. December won't need her human memories for her bird life."*

Adrian grabs a tissue from the box next to my hospital bed and wipes the tears from his eyes. I've never seen him cry.

"You can stop." I take another sip of the slushy. My tongue is probably blue, an iridescent blue that would never be found in nature. "I wanted you to read that, and to tell you I don't believe that anymore. And I'm not . . . I want you to remember that even if we end up living in the forest somewhere, I want to be with Eleanor. I've never said that about any foster parent before, so you have to know I'm serious, right?"

Adrian closes *Bird Girl*. He pats my hand. "I know you're serious."

"Always remember that, okay?" I tell him again.

"Don't worry, December, I'll remember," he says, and the door closes.

The room is quiet. Adrian will remember what I said to him today, and I'll always remember that I have it in me to survive anything.

22

In Eleanor's truck, the heater is running full blast, and I sink into the seat. The warm air feels good.

We drive down the road. Christmas lights have a faded glow, and the sound of the heater coming through vents is almost better than listening to Eleanor sing, but not quite.

"I don't know where you were planning on going right now," I say to Eleanor, "but can you take me to see Henrietta?"

"You're feeling up to it?"

"I've missed her. I want to take her out. I want to start training her again."

Since one of my wrists is broken, I use the other arm for Henrietta. She's in good spirits, like she's happy to see me, and she hops right onto the glove. "I'm glad I'm here, too," I tell her.

I carry her out to the field, and she climbs onto the perch.

We walk about fifteen yards from her. Eleanor places raw meat on my glove, and I move my hand up and down, ringing the bell hanging from my wrist. Henrietta spreads her wings, but doesn't take flight.

"Give her a second," Eleanor says.

I'll give her as much time as she needs. I needed time, too, to accept the truth about my story, to know I can't erase the reason I have a scar on my back.

Watching Henrietta take flight, flying right at me, is worth the wait.

"Good job, Henrietta," I tell her as she pecks at the meat.

The rest of Henrietta's flights are strong, and when we get into the truck, I'm happy. Eleanor starts the ignition.

"So, where are we going now?" I ask.

"Home."

"I thought we didn't have a home."

Eleanor smiles and sings "Eleanor Rigby" louder than I've ever heard her sing.

She turns down the driveway to her old house. The first time Adrian brought me here, I didn't believe I was going to stay for more than a few days.

"Wait in the truck. I'll be right back."

From here the tips of my flight tree's branches shiver in the wind, like they're waving goodbye, and through cracks in the fence I see pieces of the garden, a little bit of gray from one of the birdbaths.

Eleanor slides a box into the bed of the truck.

"You ready to see our new house?" she says.

"You're leaving your garden?"

"Guess I am. At our new house, there's a spot where we can start one. It's not as big a space, but it's big enough for us."

Us, we, our. These words don't seem so far away. Maybe the words, no matter where I go in this world, will always be a little strange for me. But they almost feel normal.

Our house is still out in the country, but it's closer to the river. It's a shade of blue gray I would call *slate*, with a rust-colored trim. The door is painted rust, too.

Eleanor unlocks the door.

I've lived in houses where everything had a place, houses where things were scattered everywhere, and houses that were in between. I've never lived in a house where I got to choose where things went, where I got to start from a beginning.

The best part about the house is it has a deck in the backyard. There's a little grass below, then the yard drops off a bluff, leading to the river. Tree branches cut the sunset sky into delicate pieces.

I lean over the edge of the railing as far as I can go. A robin flutters its wings across the grass, flying into the line of trees. There's a gate on the balcony, opening to a set of stairs that lead down to the backyard and out to the bluff.

Looking up through cottonwoods, I want to see if I can stare at the sky without thinking of flight. My eyes don't stay on the blue for long, and I focus on the trees, following branches to where they meet the trunk, then following the trunk down to where it's secured to the ground, by roots. In the distance there's the sound of real birds taking flight, or it's the sound of the river, or it's just the wind, growing stronger, strong enough to blow away a story I don't want to tell anymore.

"You want to see your room?" Eleanor asks.

There are only two bedrooms in the house. Eleanor turns on the light, and says, "Surprise!" The room is bare except for blue origami birds from my birthday, and the pink ones we made at the hospital, hanging from the ceiling.

"You can take them down anytime."

I lean into Eleanor. "I'm going to keep them up forever."

"I have a feeling in a couple years you'll be tired of them. Not the fact they're birds"—Eleanor rests her arm around my shoulders—"but the color. You'll probably want to replace them with black birds." She squeezes me against her.

"Maybe I'll replace them with ravens. They're fierce birds. Smart, too."

"Fierce and smart is always good." Eleanor kisses me on the forehead. "I brought some soup for dinner from the other house, and bought some bread. And I grabbed your bag of sunflower seeds."

"I'm going to try dinner without sunflower seeds tonight."

"Okay, I'll unwrap some bowls and some spoons, then."

The gas stove clicks as Eleanor lights one of the burners. I stare at the origami birds. They're still, no air moving them back and forth. These birds are a lot more like me.

I watch Eleanor lay a blanket in the middle of the living room floor, where we'll eat dinner. She ladles soup into each of our bowls. Funny, maybe I don't know everything about her yet, but I feel like I've known her all my life. In all the foster homes I've lived, deep down I was really waiting for the houses to turn into my home, but they never did. They were more like nests, there to give me shelter until I needed to fly.

I sit down on the blanket and stir the soup with a spoon.

The sense of sight is most important to a bird's survival. Birds' perception of color is much better than humans'. They see different spectrums of light and can detect violet and some ultraviolet wavelengths. Humans can detect red, blue, and green wavelengths. But we can also survive without seeing.

I see the soup's broth is yellow. The potatoes and leeks float on the surface.

The sense of smell is more developed in some birds than others. The turkey vulture has a keen sense of smell so it can locate decaying flesh. But humans rely on this sense much more than birds do.

I smell the leeks and a little bit of lavender soap.

Birds have a poor sense of taste. Maybe that's why they don't mind worms. Humans, though, have about ten thousand taste buds. Birds have fewer than one hundred. But birds can still recognize flavors and do have their favorite foods.

I dip my spoon into the soup and catch a potato. I sip first. It's warm. It's salty. It's good. I bite down on the potato. It holds the flavor of the soup. I take another bite.

The range of a bird's hearing is similar to humans'. They hear sounds differently. They also can hear shorter sounds than humans can.

Between the sounds of me sipping soup, I hear Eleanor humming. She's standing by the toaster oven, warming bread. She's not humming "Eleanor Rigby." It's a different song. I'll ask her later what song it is. The toaster oven makes a *ding* sound. Outside, on the porch, chimes ring.

Eleanor sits down and spreads butter on bread. Behind her, through a window, tree branches cut the almost-dark sky into triangular pieces. If I looked long and hard enough, I'm sure I'd find an outline of a bird's wing.

"The soup is good."

Eleanor smiles. I don't know if my mom ever smiled at me. She must've, at least once, maybe when I was first born when the nurse laid me in her arms. Holding me then was the easy part, though.

But it doesn't matter now.

23

It's harder to see the sky from the deck. Heart-shaped leaves block my view.

"You ready to go?" Eleanor asks.

On the way to school, the first song we always sing is "Eleanor Rigby." I know the words by heart.

The song isn't yet over when Eleanor stops in front of the school, but I keep singing until the end.

"Have a good day," Eleanor says.

I give her a thumbs-up and a wave goodbye.

At lunch recess, Cheryllynn and I sit under a tree at the far end of the playground. She opens *The Complete Guide to Birds: Volume One*. "Page two hundred ninety-four."

"Toucans!" I throw my arms in the air.

Cheryllynn laughs, and then yells, "Let's hear it for toucans!"

"They can't fly very far, and the look of their bill is

deceptive. It looks heavy, but it's really very light because it's made of a spongy substance called keratin—the same thing our hair and nails are made of. Its bill is good for reaching fruit on trees, or reaching down into holes for insects, but because it isn't strong, it's not effective to use against predators."

I see the Vultures coming across the grass. Today, they're all wearing pink from head to toe.

"They really could leave us alone if they wanted to," Cheryllynn says. "They don't deserve to wear pink." She stands up. "Pink wasn't made for mean people."

We walk toward the girls and meet them in the middle of the field. They surround us, just like vultures do. I don't see Matilda—maybe she's absent today.

"What do you want, Jenny?" Cheryllynn shoves her hands in the pocket of her furry coat.

"What did you do to your hair?" Jenny points at me. "It looks like a pile of sticks."

"Yeah, it looks like a nest," one of the other girls says. "Looks like you would have a hard time even combing it. It looks . . ."

"Her hair is fine." Cheryllynn takes a step toward Jenny. "You never used to be mean. Where'd that person go?"

Jenny folds her arms in front of her chest and stares at the ground. She doesn't have an answer, and turns around, the rest of the group following her.

"My hair might look like a nest," I yell, "but for your information, birds take building nests very seriously. If you've ever looked at a nest up close, they're beautiful, intricate, and detailed. Like my hair."

The Vultures don't look back, don't have anything to say. I guess they are evolving.

Across the playground, Matilda stands next to the fence, by a tree, with her hands in her coat pockets. She is here today. I wave. She waves, too. She doesn't seem to be a part of Jenny's group anymore.

"You were glorious, you know?" Cheryllynn says.

"And you"—I rest my arm around her shoulders—"are extraordinary."

After school, I have an appointment with Dr. S. I sit across from her.

"How is your wrist?" she asks. Not a *why* question.

"Still a little sore."

"And how is your heart?"

An unusual question for Dr. S. She's never mentioned my heart before. "It's fine." And it is, no abnormal heartbeats or rhythms. "It moves about eighty beats per minute." I'm not sure where she's going with her questions, but I've decided to answer them in a practical way. No half-truths.

Dr. S is wearing a blue scarf with blue pants that match,

and a white blouse that would be terrible for camouflage unless she was an emperor penguin living in Antarctica. Her white belly would help her hide from predators like the leopard seal. The seals would look up and the white would blend in with light coming through the water's surface.

"I have a *why* question for *you* today."

"Ask away."

"Why did you just ask me how my heart was?"

"Well, I'm an admirer of Amelia Earhart, too. One of my favorite quotes of hers is, 'Everyone has oceans to fly, if they have the heart to do it.' The rest of the quote is . . ."

" 'Is it reckless? Maybe, but what do dreams know of boundaries?' "

"That's right."

Dr. S carries my backpack out to the waiting room. Eleanor folds a magazine about taxidermy into her purse.

"We had a very good session," Dr. S tells her. "She's making very good progress."

Even though the scar on my back will always be there, I feel like I'm making progress, too.

On our way out of the office, Eleanor says, "And now, we have a bird to visit."

At the rehabilitation center, I can tell by Henrietta's squawk that she's stronger today. Her pitch is fierce. It has fight in it. Inside the cage she's perched on a branch, her eyes following our movements.

"I think she's ready to try to fly on her own." Eleanor hands me the falconry glove. "Let's see what she can do."

Eleanor opens the cage, and I hold the glove out to Henrietta. "Today is going to be your day."

Behind the rehabilitation center there's a field. Beyond the field is the line of trees growing by the river.

"Now, she might take to this free thing, or she might not. In case she does, do you want to say anything to her first?" Eleanor asks.

I'm all out of Amelia Earhart quotes, and telling Henrietta what I know about birds, how I think they're the most beautiful animals on earth, seems pointless. She knows what she is. She knows what she has to do. Her main purpose: survive. But even birds need a little luck, a little help from someone sometimes.

Eleanor leans her head close to Henrietta and says, "You're strong, but if you need more time, we're here." She looks at me. "Right, December?"

"Right," I whisper.

"On three," Eleanor says.

One. All animals need a place to call home.

Two. All animals need parents, even if it's just for the purpose of coming into this world.

Three. All animals need one another, whether we realize it or not.

I swoop my arm up in the air, but Henrietta clings to the glove.

"If you can, thrust your arm more up and out to give her a little momentum," Eleanor says.

I do, but Henrietta doesn't want to let go. "Is she afraid?"

"No," Eleanor says, "she just doesn't want to say goodbye." She leans close to Henrietta. "We don't want to say goodbye, either, but the world is waiting for you." She turns to me. "Let's try something else. Take off your glove."

Eleanor holds Henrietta for me. "When you throw her up in the air, you're going to have to completely let go. You think you can do it? If you want, I can . . ."

"No." I want to be the one to set Henrietta free.

"When you thrust her into the air"—Eleanor demonstrates the technique with her arms—"it's going to feel awkward, and she might flutter her wings and land on the ground."

"If she does," I say, "we'll try again, right?"

"You bet." Eleanor nods and smiles.

"Okay, girl," I whisper to Henrietta, "this is it."

I don't think. I don't count. I throw Henrietta into the air, and let go. She doesn't flutter, or hesitate. She flies a short distance to a tree, landing on one of the branches.

"She's just getting a feel for where she is," Eleanor says.

Minutes pass and Henrietta still hasn't moved. "Maybe she's having second thoughts about leaving."

But right after I say "leaving," Henrietta proves me wrong and takes flight. She flies above the field and circles around it, soaring over Eleanor and me, and swoops toward the river, standing out against spring's shades of green.

And that's it. She's free.

There's a bench against the building, and Eleanor sits down on it, closing her eyes and lifting her face to the sun. "Henrietta was my tenth bird I've set free. I'll never get tired of it. And I'll never get tired of having you around. I promise."

"We'll see," I say. These words belong to the bird girl, December, words still filled with fear and caution. But maybe it's a good thing I still need for people to prove their words to me. Even Eleanor.

"Yes, you will see," she says.

Birds have memory. Some can scatter seeds across many miles and remember where they placed them. Songbirds remember songs they were taught when they were young. In a test, some pigeons were able to memorize twelve hundred pictures.

No matter what, for as long as I live, I'll always remember the words to "Eleanor Rigby," the way Eleanor sings it, low and kind of sad, but with a smile across her face, like there's a lot of hope in the sadness. That's what I love about her.

Against the sky, a handful of blackbirds swoop through blue, catching currents of wind, moving in and out of sunlight. I am a human. I am a girl. I don't know how long I'll have to keep saying this to myself, but I will.

A bird's life, as any animal's, is about surviving. They fly, they migrate, they eat, they lay eggs, they sleep. Humans are animals. Our main purpose is the same as a bird's, but in between migrating, eating, sleeping, fighting, we laugh, cry, talk, yell, make each other feel happy and feel sad. Our survival is a lot more complicated. Some of our lives are easier, some more gnarled. That's the nature of us. Of Cheryllynn, of Eleanor. Of me.

My name is December Lee Morgan. The scar on my back isn't where wings once unfolded. It's where bones and blood are etched with only a part of my story.

I think birds are the most amazing creatures on earth. What sets them apart is their ability to fly on their own.

ACKNOWLEDGMENTS

Finding and honing December's story was a long journey, and there were many people who chose to take the journey with me—I will be forever grateful to all of you.

First, I want to thank my agent, Patricia Nelson. She is intelligent, passionate, and so, so kind. Thank you for believing in me, and in December, and for always being there.

I want to thank Joanna Marple for her time and insight into earlier drafts of this book. Thank you, too, for your friendship. During the Nevada SCBWI mentor program in 2012, Susan Hart Lindquist said to me, "I think you should write middle grade." I started writing *Extraordinary Birds* not too long after. Thanks for that piece of wisdom, Susan. I'm glad I took your advice.

To my editor, Allison Moore, thank you so much for "getting" December, for your brilliance in making her story stronger, and for your enthusiasm and dedication in bringing December's voice into the wider world. I feel so lucky to have you in my corner.

Thank you to the entire team at Bloomsbury, especially Anna Bernard, Lizzy Mason, Erica Barmash, Beth Eller, Brittany Mitchell, Alona Fryman, Valentina Rice, Cristina Gilbert, Jeanette Levy, Donna Mark, Yelena Safronova, Liz Byer, Diane Aronson, Melissa Kavonic, Nick Sweeney, Cindy Loh, Annette Pollert-Morgan, Nicholas Church, Zoe Griffiths, Jo Blaquiere, Alice Grigg, Joanna Everard, Rosie Ahmed, Frank Bumbalo, and the sales team. I'm amazed by your support and love for this story.

Thank you to Leo Nickolls for his beautiful cover showing December in a new light.

I'd also like to thank Trevor Davis for taking time to answer any questions I had about California's foster care system, and Sydney Fowler for their insight into Cheryllynn.

Lastly, thank you to my family. To Constance and to my sister, Tami, for always reminding me of what I was capable of doing with my writing. To my mom, who taught me to "just keep going." And, to my husband, who has weathered many of my dark clouds, but remained, as he still does, the sunlight.

AUTHOR'S NOTE

There's always one student who walks into my classroom on the first day of school and seems quieter than the rest. There's something about them that says they've experienced something tough—the way they whisper when they talk, the way they keep their head down, doing anything they can to avoid being noticed. They come to school every day carrying scars that aren't visible.

Students like this, and stories I read in the newspaper about difficult family situations, were the seeds that inspired December. Throughout the book, she finds a way to get through her own life's letdowns, using her deep passion for birds and weaving a tale about how she will become one. But she comes to realize that sometimes the stories we tell ourselves in order to survive can actually make our scars deeper. In searching for a place where she can build enough trust to accept the truth of what happened to her, December discovers there are people in the world who will be there for her when she falls.

Other students in my class, young people who bravely asserted who they were inside, were the inspiration for Cheryllynn, and some of my favorite adults were the inspiration for Eleanor. *Extraordinary Birds* is, among other things, a story about community, about finding a place that embraces you for who you are without any judgment. It is a story about everyday kids and adults choosing to live their lives with hope, honesty, and compassion. It is a story that I hope celebrates young people's lives in all their complexities.

In my classroom, we love to discuss stories that inspire us to see the world differently. I hope this book does the same.

Thank you for reading.

READER DISCUSSION GUIDE

Sandy Stark-McGinnis is also a teacher who loves discussing books with students. If you'd like to discuss *Extraordinary Birds* with your class or book group, here are some suggestions for questions and writing prompts.

Discussion Questions:

- What was your first impression of December? Did you think she believed she would really transform into a bird? Why or why not?

- Why do you think Eleanor and Cheryllynn are able to understand December? How does this help her trust them?

- What feelings did the relationship between December and Cheryllynn evoke in you? Why do you think the author chose to create this relationship?

- Cheryllynn has her own obstacles to navigate. What characteristics does she have that allow her to be confident and stand up to the Vultures?

- What do you think motivates Jenny's feelings toward Cheryllynn?

- Which character did you identify with the most? Did they remind you of anyone in your own life?

- For what reasons, other than her passion for birds, do you think December shares bird facts?

- Why does December choose orange to describe the sound of Karen's voice?

- What parallels are there between December and Henrietta, and between December and Teresa?

- What is the purpose of December's *Bird Girl* story?

- There is a danger in December jumping out of trees. Why do you believe she risks the possibility of getting hurt?

- What adjectives would you use to describe the way December feels at the end of the story when she releases Henrietta?

- How does the last line of the book relate to December and what she has learned living with Eleanor?

- What do you think the future holds for December? For Cheryllynn? For Eleanor?

Writing Prompts:

- Write a poem expressing how December feels on her way to Eleanor's house for the first time.

- Write a journal entry from December's point of view after she releases Henrietta.

- Pretend it's a year after the story ends. Write a letter to December from Henrietta's point of view, telling her about your life since being released back into the wild.

- Choose two birds. Research facts about them (habitat, diet, behavior, and anything else you find interesting). Analyze your data and compare and contrast the two birds. Based on your research, which bird is most similar to you? Why?

"The desert's beautiful," she says. It is.

She turns back, staring at me like I'm the sky. "I know you're my daughter. But I can't remember your name." She holds my face in her hands and presses her forehead against mine, staring into my eyes, searching for "Cassie."

She's been forgetting names of things a lot lately. Like, she'll know a brush is used for fixing your hair but can't remember the word to identify it. Last week, she asked me, "What is that thing you use for writing?"

I found a pencil and a pen. I held up the pencil and said, "This is a pencil." I held up the pen and said, "This is a pen." Mom chose the pen, and then I helped her make a grocery list for Dad.

When she can't remember the name of something, she

describes it to me. "It's a vegetable. It's green. It looks like it has short, dark green hair." Broccoli.

My name is like "pen," "pencil," "broccoli." Except it's not.

I almost say, "This person loves art. She loves to go on hikes. She loves you." But I don't. I can't.

"I'm Cassie." I barely get out the words.

Cassie, I think. *You used to say how beautiful it was. You used to tell me all the time.* And now she can't remember it.

A tear rolls down my cheek. The wind, shaking sagebrush across the desert floor, feels colder. My throat hurts. It's trying to hold the sadness away, sadness mixed with anger, mixed with a wide-open feeling that there isn't anything I, my dad, or even the doctors can do to stop my mom from losing herself. Her memory is like the desert in front of us, formed by tiny particles of mountain broken down into smaller and smaller pieces, becoming sand, then pieces of sand breaking down so tiny, they don't exist anymore.

Except, in the desert, it seems like there are always more pieces of sand to replace those that are lost. Once Mom loses a memory, it sometimes doesn't come back. So the chances of her ever remembering my name again aren't good.

"Isn't it beautiful?" she says again.

No. Nothing is beautiful. How can she say that when

she can't remember my name? My name is beautiful, remember? She's the one who gave it to me. How could she forget?

I want to scream across the "beautiful" desert, but I have to remind myself that Mom can't help what's happening to her.

I take a deep breath, trying to swallow my tears, and bend down to collect some rocks. I use my hand to scrape the ground, making the dirt flat and more compact, and use the rocks to spell out my name. If I had paint, I'd paint them blue, ocean blue, so Mom could get lost in the letters.

"See." I press myself against her and feel her warmth, erasing the cold wind for a second.

I'm hoping she'll read the word, but instead she takes a last drink of her root beer and kisses me on the nose. "I love you."

That should be enough. *I love you.*

But on the way back to the house, I can't help but repeat "Cassie" over and over again, the rhythm of my name dictating our steps.

Saying it out loud probably won't help her remember my name. But I need to hear it. Sometimes I need help, too.

"Cassie." Dad's waiting for us inside the doorway. "Where did you go?"

Mom slips under his arm into the house and leaves the empty root beer bottle on the porch.

"Mom wanted to go for a walk, and I followed her."

He doesn't like that answer. "I'm going to tell you again. We can't let her walk out the door on her own. It makes our lives harder. Okay?"

I nod. I agree that Mom escaping and going outside does make our lives harder, but I can't blame her for wanting to escape.

I get that he's afraid. I am, too. But our fears have different degrees, different angles and values when it comes to Mom. I'm afraid we won't have time to do and say everything we need to before we have to say goodbye.

Sometimes Dad's fears really have to do with how people would react to Mom if we did take her places, but he says he's just focused on keeping her safe.

This is the complete opposite of our life before Mom got sick. We would go places all the time, hiking, camping, taking trips to the beach.

"We just went for a walk, Dad. That's all. I stayed with her the whole time. Everything was fine." I grab the root beer bottle and go to my room.

I shove the bottle and my math book into my backpack. "Cassie," I whisper. "It's Cassie."

On a shelf, there's a container with small plastic dolphins

that Mom gave me last year for Christmas. I grab three, not caring what kinds of dolphins they are, and shove them inside my jeans' pocket.

There's a knock on the front door. "Good morning!" Mrs. Collins says.

It's not a good morning.

On the way to school, it starts to rain. The radio plays; Dad's listening to the news. I swear I hear the newswoman say, "Up next, a story about a woman who can't remember her own daughter's name."

Mom was the one who used to drive me to school and pick me up. I miss my rides with her. She was good at making the twenty minutes fun.

"So," Dad says, "do you want to have spaghetti for dinner tonight?"

"That's fine."

"Spaghetti's your favorite."

"It is."

From the car window, I can see the mountains. They're a shade of red, like the ones Georgia O'Keeffe painted. I've been saving my money to go to Santa Fe and visit her museum. It would be nice to get lost in her red cliffs and *The Lawrence Tree* or hide behind cow skulls or inside one of her sunflower paintings.

Dad pulls up in front of Desert Valley Elementary School. I get out, lift my too-heavy backpack from the back seat, and close the door.

"Cassie?" He says my name like a question. He's been doing this a lot since Mom got sick. I get it, though. I feel unsure about a lot of things now, too. Questions and the unknown are our new normal.

I lean against the open window.

"Is something wrong?"

"No."

"Okay." Of course, Dad knows there's something wrong, something besides just Mom, and he says *okay* because he thinks if he doesn't pressure me about it, I'll be more likely to tell him. But I don't want to say anything. He has enough to worry about.

"Have a good day," he says.

I wave goodbye. A "good day" would look like this: walking through the door when I get home and Mom saying, "Cassie, did you do your homework?" or, "Cassie, please clean up your room," or, "Cassie, will you take out the garbage?"

Or just, "Cassie."

SWIMMING THE ENGLISH CHANNEL

The wind is perfect, and we're the only ones on the beach.

"You ready to run?" Dad asks.

Mom gives me the reel. "You're ready."

But I know how much she loves to fly kites. "You first."

"Together." She grins and takes my hand.

Behind us, Dad holds the kite in the air. "You'll go on three."

Against my feet, the sand is cool. I usually look ahead and try to listen to Dad give directions, but Mom runs with her eyes on the kite. I don't know how she does it. Lots of practice, maybe? Or a trust that her feet are going to land where they're supposed to, even if she isn't focused on planting them with each step.

"Let's give it some slack, Cassie," she says.

I roll more string out from the reel and try to look up at the kite, too. My feet stumble a little, and I fall, letting go of the string on my way down. Mom holds on and keeps running.

"You okay?" Her voice travels down the beach.

"I'm fine." I am, except for a little taste of sunscreen in my mouth. (Mom says, with our pale skin, we need to be extra careful.) I don't bother getting up and open my eyes to the sky. There's no sun to shield them from, and I can watch the clouds. They're moving fast today.

Pretty soon, her shoulder is right beside mine. "Okay, what ocean animals do you see?" She points up at one of the clouds, to the left of the kite, still flying. "That's definitely a stingray."

I can't make out the outline of a stingray at all. "I don't see it."

"Keep looking. It's there."

I try to find it but can't. "You know, the truth is, I usually can't find half the things you say you see in the clouds." I laugh.

"Well, Cassie." Mom raises up on her elbows, leans over, and gives me a kiss on the cheek. "The truth is, I make up half the things I say I see in the clouds."

I smile. "I know."

She lies back down, grabs my hand, and sets it over her heart, while her other hand holds the reel. "I guess it's not exactly telling the truth, is it? It's nice of you to play along."

"It is nice of me, huh?"

Mom giggles. "I do it for a good reason, and I suppose you know what the reason is, too?"

"Maybe because you want to keep the game going longer?"

I wait for her to tell me whether I'm right, but Dad walks up. "You want me to take the kite?" he asks.

"No, I got it." Mom stares up at the colors. The kite bobs and weaves with the wind, but for the most part, it stays steady.

Last year in math class, Mrs. Jones, my teacher, asked us if we could identify characteristics of a kite. *They're different colors and different shapes.* That's all I knew. When she started talking about adjacent and perpendicular lines, I understood what she was teaching us, but I didn't want to think too much about it. Because I like to think of kites the way Mom does: *an extension of our arms. With them, we can touch the sky.*

"Dad, do you see a stingray in the clouds?" I ask him, pointing to where Mom did earlier.

Mom laughs.

"I know that trick," Dad says.

The reel of the kite drops onto her stomach, but then the wind scoots it across the beach toward the ocean. All of us get up and run after it. By the time we reach the reel, the kite has tumbled onto the sand, the tide washing over it. Mom picks it up by the frame.

"Not much use now," I say.

"I don't know." She shakes the kite gently. "Let's dry it out and see what happens. It's always worth a try."

"It's not going to . . ." Dad stops himself from saying "work" because Mom's giving him a look. It's one she gives me when I'm about to complain about getting a B on a math test.

I know what she's going to say next. It's her answer for pretty much everything, and she says it in a soft voice that sounds even quieter compared to the waves. "Let's go get some ice cream. We can talk about how we're going to get this kite back up into the air over a sundae."

Dad says he'll meet us at the car.

Before leaving, it's my and Mom's tradition to always say goodbye to the ocean. "Until next time," she says, and waves to the water between us and the horizon. "I'm always amazed at how big it is."

"Me too." We lift our feet out of the damp sand and move closer to the water. "How far do you think you'd be able to swim out before you started to get scared?"

"Pretty far."

Even though the water would be cold, Mom would keep swimming. She'd only stop if she got hungry or thirsty.

"What about you?" she asks as she holds my hand.

"Not very far." I'm a good swimmer, but I don't like swimming in the ocean.

"Why not?"

"It's scary. All that space around you, and it's dark and unpredictable."

" 'Unpredictable.' That's a big word."

"That's why I like math. Numbers. They have a pattern."

Mom laughs. "Patterns are good, but what if 'unpredictable' leads to amazing adventures?"

"If I had to jump in the ocean first to get to that adventure, well, I'd rather sit down on the beach and do long division all day."

A car horn sounds. Dad's waving for us to *come on*. "Ice cream!" he yells. "Rocky road! Orange sherbet! Chocolate chip!" Each flavor one of our favorites.

"We better go."

Mom points to the sky. "There's a dolphin."

The cloud does have a dolphin-like shape to it. "I see it this time," I say.

She moves her foot back and forth across the sand.

"What's the longest distance you've ever swam?" I ask her.

"I'm not sure. But one day I'm going to swim the English Channel," she says. Mom loves big ideas. I haven't heard this plan before, but I'm not too surprised.

"Maybe by then you'll see the water in a different

way . . . or maybe you'll still think it's scary. But it doesn't matter . . . unless you want to join me."

"I don't think so," I say.

"That's okay. Because when I swim it, I'll need a support crew!" She nods and gives me a wink. "You're good at reading charts and data, so you can be in charge of reporting any rough weather or crazy currents that could push me off course."

I laugh as we grab our flip-flops.

SANDY STARK-McGINNIS is the author of *Extraordinary Birds* and *The Space Between Lost and Found*. She is also an award-winning poet and holds an MA in creative writing from San Francisco State University. Sandy lives with her husband and children in California, where she works as a fifth-grade teacher.

www.sandystarkmcginnis.com
@McGinnisSandy